Wycliffe
AND
DEATH IN A SALUBRIOUS PLACE

W.J.Burley

An Orion paperback

First published in Great Britain in 1973
by Victor Gollancz Ltd
First published in paperback in 1976
by Arrow
This paperback edition published in 2005
by Orion Books,
an imprint of the Orion Publishing Group Ltd,
Orion House, 5 Upper St Martin's Lane,
London WC2H 9EA

An Hachette UK company

5 7 9 10 8 6

A CIP catalogue record for this book is available
from the British Library.

ISBN 978-0-7528-6535-5

Printed and bound in Great Britain by
Clays Ltd, St Ives plc

www.orionbooks.co.uk

To David Dearlove

in appreciation of his kindness
in allowing me to use
one of his songs

Chapter One

Sylvie died without knowing why. In the instant when she had realized his intention and before the blow fell, when it was already too late to make the smallest effort to escape, she had experienced not only a paralysing fear but profound astonishment. It is said of some who die by violence that their features express neither horror nor fear but only intense surprise. Had it been possible to discern any expression on the battered face of the girl it might well have been one of blank incredulity. She died because she had not listened, because she was indifferent.

For twenty minutes the man had walked beside her when, above all else, she wanted to be alone. With the masochistic self-indulgence of deeply injured pride she wanted only to relive the moment, probe the wound, extract the last scrap of pain and humiliation from the experience. But she had not wanted to die. Even in the depths of her misery a small voice whispered that it would pass. A tiny part of her mind was beginning to make healing adjustments; even, perhaps, to skirmish with the practical problems which would now confront her. At heart, she was a realist.

It was late. Overhead, in a cloudless sky, the stars were brilliant points of cold light. Nearer the horizon they twinkled through thickening mists. The landscape in the starlight was pale, almost bleached.

They had climbed the slope out of the valley. Salubrious Place was behind them, two or three lights, orange rectangles, tawdry compared with the pure light of the stars. Without thinking about it she saw him stoop and pick up a sort of bar with a loop at one end. The area around the quarry was littered with odds and ends of scrap from the machinery which had once been used to work it. He liked to have something in his hand when he walked over the downs. Usually it was a stick and he would cut and slash at the brambles bordering the path like a destructive small boy.

They walked, picking their way round the big stones, avoiding the pot-holes but they saw almost nothing, their consciousness was not involved. His voice punctuated the silence. Intense, soft, sometimes stung to anger by her failure to respond. To her, with her present preoccupation, it was no more demanding of attention than the sound of waves breaking lazily on the beach or the mournful tolling of the bell-buoy out to sea.

Then, suddenly, her attention was arrested, but it was too late, she did not even raise a hand to ward off the blow. She crumpled. It is possible that he delivered another blow while she lay on the ground but afterwards he could not remember. Perhaps he stood over her for a time, certainly he was stunned. Then he heard voices and laughter, for a moment he could not remember where he was or what had happened, it was like waking from a vivid dream. But memory came flooding back and he realized that he still held the iron bar with its looped end. He threw it away from him with all the energy he could muster and heard it clatter, metal against metal; perhaps it had fallen into the quarry, striking one of the rusting, broken trucks which were strewn over the quarry floor among the boulders. So much the better. He rubbed his hand vigorously against his jacket.

The voices were getting closer; they had finished their session at the Barn and were on their way home. In a couple of minutes they would be with him. He stooped and lifted Sylvie's body. It was a struggle. Her weight surprised and dismayed him. For a moment he swayed and almost fell with her but he managed to stumble away from the track through a gap in the brambles and gorse. In a small clearing he rested, trying to control his breathing and the beating of his heart. They were level with him now, shouting, laughing absurdly, jostling each other. Ten yards away but more remote than the mountains of the moon. Their footsteps and their voices died away at last.

He had another ten or fifteen yards to go. For the first time he noticed the mist drifting in from the sea, eddying, swirling, dispersing. He must try again. He put out his hand and touched a warm stickiness which made him want to vomit. He had been careful not to look at her head and face, now, accidentally, he had touched. He rubbed his hand on the short turf. He had carried her so that her head was well away from his clothing but it was still possible . . . He took off his jacket and placed it carefully on the ground then he bent to lift her once more. He would have dragged her body to the quarry but already his instinct for self-preservation was at work. If he could get her to the quarry without leaving too many traces her death might be put down to accident. He knew the weather in the islands, this mist would thicken to fog in a short while and it might then be supposed that she had lost her way.

Another effort which taxed his strength to the limit and he had her body more or less securely over his shoulder. He tottered the distance to the quarry edge, dropped her to the ground for fear of being carried over with her. He had a dread of heights. With his foot, he gently propelled her body to the very edge then kicked vigorously. It seemed a long time before he heard a splash and a muffled thud. She had fallen in the water and soft mud which lay at the foot of the quarry face.

He walked back to where he had left his jacket but before putting it on he took off his shirt and rolled it inside out, just in case. His jacket felt cold and damp against his naked body. He was trembling and shivering at the same time.

All through the summer night the islands had been blanketed in sea fog and measured bleats of the signals on Temple Rock and on Ship Island had punctuated the moist silence, blending in a complex rhythm. Now it was full daylight, a diffused opalescent brilliance from no apparent source revealing a tiny world of gorse and bracken.

'She'll clear directly.'

Two men in reefer jackets and sea boots trudged along a stony track.

'We're wasting our time, Matt, until she clears a bit.' He spoke almost pleadingly but the other man seemed not to hear.

The two men represented contrasted island types: Matthew Eva, thickset, powerful, blond, with thinning, curly hair and a ruddy complexion; Jack Bishop, thin, small-boned, dark and sallow. The lion and the jackal.

'There's nothing can have happened to her, Matt. She'll have lost her way in the fog and decided to sit it out somewhere. Your Sylvie's a sensible girl, got her head screwed on. She'll be on her way home by now.'

'You reckon?' Matt was cynical, not consoled.

Moisture stood out in little beads on their jackets and glistened on their features like sweat.

Suddenly, magically, the curtain of mist lifted and their range of vision increased from a few yards to a mile or more. They could see the rough moorland sloping away to the sea on their left and to their right, Carngluze, a rugged outcrop of granite, the highest point in the islands, emerged spectrally from the mist and was lost again.

'There!' Jack Bishop said as though he had contrived the miracle himself.

For more than an hour they quartered the rough ground. The mist still hid the carn and there was a grey, impenetrable wall not far offshore. There was no sign of Morvyl or Biddock nor any hint of the Western Rocks. From time to time they stopped and shouted, their voices small, 'Sylvie! Sylvie!'

'We'd best get back and if she isn't home we can get together a party and make a proper search . . .'

'I'm going to look in the quarry.'

'The quarry? She wouldn't have had any call to go near the quarry.'

But Matt was already ploughing through a thicket of gorse.

The quarry had been cut and blasted out of the side of the carn to provide material for almost all the buildings on the island which antedated the era of the concrete block. Now it was deserted with the rusty stanchions of a derrick, a giant winch and the corroding shell of a steam boiler, as monuments to an age that was gone.

The two men stood on the lip of the quarry with the granite face dropping sheer for thirty or forty feet below them. At the bottom brambles grew among the rusting bogies of overturned tram-trucks and, nearer the face, there was a pool of grey-green water fringed with some kind of rush.

'There she is.' Matt spoke seemingly without surprise or emotion as though he had only found what he expected to find.

A girl in a red wet-look mackintosh, her body curiously twisted, was lying in the rushes, her face in the water, her blonde hair floating like weeds. 'My God!' Jack Bishop whispered.

They followed round the edge of the quarry to where a tram-track ran down a steep slope to the floor. Their sea boots slipped and slithered on loose gravel and once they were down they had to scramble over the bramble-covered debris of granite blocks and scrap iron which littered the ground. When they bent over the girl they were standing in several inches of soft grey mud. They lifted her and carried her clear of the rushes then laid her on a granite slab which was more or less flat.

Matthew Eva looked down at his daughter, his china-blue eyes hard and cold. There could be no possible doubt that she was dead, the frontal bones of the skull and her facial bones had been splintered inwards like the cracked shell of an egg.

It was not the first time the two men had encountered violent death; wrecks, drownings and cliff falls marked the calendar of the islands. All the same . . .

She was blond, like her father, and her skin, where it was undamaged, was delicate and translucent. Under her mackintosh she wore a white blouse and a tartan pinafore dress. Jack Bishop looked from her to the rim of the quarry and back again finding no words for the emotion he felt. All he could say was, 'She must've mistook her way in the fog and just walked over . . .'

'Don't give me that!' The intensity of anger in Matt's voice frightened him. 'You fetch Freddie Jordan, I'm stopping here.' Freddie Jordan was a sergeant of police, the law in the islands.

The sun was winning the battle overhead and by the time Bishop got to the top of the ramp he was sweating. He glanced back once and saw that Matt had covered his daughter's body with his coat. It was two miles to the town and when he reached the slopes above the bay the church bell was tolling for Holy Communion. Eight o'clock. Sunday morning.

A perfect crescent of sand stretched for a mile beyond the town, white in the sun; the sprawl of grey houses and the patchwork of lichen-covered roofs reached up the hill towards him.

By the time Sylvie's body had been brought in and laid in the mortuary the church bells were pealing for the ten-thirty service and the pleasure boats were loading with trippers for the off-islands.

The little grey, granite police station was on the waterfront and Sergeant Jordan lived in the house next door. With the help of two constables he policed the islands under the direction of a subdivisional headquarters on the mainland. He was an islander and, on the whole, he had a soft billet. A spot of illicit salvage, a few domestics, petty thieving, and the occasional punch-up on the quay.

'My girl was murdered.'

Jordan ran his hand over his thinning and greying hair. 'You can't say that, Matt, you heard what Dr Ross . . .'

'To hell with Ross!' Matthew Eva leaned across the sergeant's desk to make his point. 'Did you see my girl's face and head?'

Jordan nodded.

'Forty feet at most that quarry is, from top to bottom, and a quagmire to fall on, soft as a feather bed . . .' He broke off as a new thought struck him, his voice fell. 'You saw my wife when they picked her up?'

Jordan nodded once more. 'I saw her.'

'Ninety feet off Cligga Head and solid rock below. Did she look like Sylvie?'

'No, Matt, she didn't, but you know as well as I do no two cases are alike. We've seen a few falls between us . . .'

'Apart from anything else,' Eva went on, ignoring the sergeant, 'is it likely that the same accident would happen to two members of the same family – mother and daughter, inside two years?' His voice had become husky with fresh grief and the sergeant spoke sympathetically.

'Believe me, Matt, you have the sympathy of everybody in the islands and from nobody more than me. There will be a full investigation. I've reported to my bosses and they'll see to that, but there's nothing more I can do.'

Eva wore no jacket and his shirt sleeves were rolled up; his massive freckled arms, covered with golden hairs, rested on the desk. He tapped the desk with a broad forefinger. 'You know as well as I do that Sylvie was murdered and that Peters killed her. If you don't do something about that, I will.'

The sergeant was provoked, he stood up. 'If I were you, Matt, I should guard my tongue; that sort of talk will do you no good and it won't bring Sylvie back. As to threats, don't force my hand. If you put a foot out of line I shall have to run you in.' His voice softened. 'Don't be a fool! We've got to do our job according to the book but that doesn't mean that it won't be done.'

Matt Eva stood up also and the two men faced each other across the desk. Eva was a head shorter than the sergeant but his was the more impressive figure. 'If that's how you want it . . .'

Jordan remained cool. 'That's how it's going to be, Matt.'

Eva snatched up his coat from a chair, slung it over his shoulder and stalked through the outer office on to the quay, leaving the door open. He stood for a moment, hesitating in the sunshine, then made off along the wharf. Once he had an idea in his head there was no shifting it. A stubborn man, a good friend and a bad enemy, liable to fits of violent temper.

The pleasure boats were on their various ways to the off-islands. A few tourists strolled in the sun, family groups trudged along with their packed lunches in the direction of the beach. M. V. *Islander* was at her berth unloading mixed cargo with her own derricks. Like any other fine Sunday in summer.

And, as on other off-duty Sundays, at twelve o'clock Matthew went into the Seymour Arms, though today he stole in furtively, feeling that what had happened should have separated him from his routine, but unable to face the aching loneliness of his empty house.

Somehow, over the years, the locals had kept the public bar of the Seymour for themselves. Through the small archway behind the bar it was possible to catch a glimpse of floral dresses and shirts, of red, peeling faces and shoulders in the saloon. And laughter and shouting provided a clamorous background to the decorous silences in the public.

Jack Bishop was playing cribbage with Charlie Martin and half a dozen other men sat on the wooden benches round the walls. They looked up as Matthew came in and acknowledged him without a word. He went to the bar, collected his drink, and took his usual seat by the window. They all knew, of course, but it would be some time before the subject was broached.

Charlie Martin was a power in the islands, he was chairman of the boat syndicate and he owned a lot of property in the island and on Morvyl. He was seventy-five, turned the scales at two hundred and fifty pounds and had the silky white hair and flowing moustaches of a biblical patriarch as well as the manner to go with them. He studied his cards through heavily lidded eyes under bushy brows. 'Four.'

'Ten.'

'Fifteen.' Charlie heaved his bulk forward to peg up two points on the board.

Jack Bishop fumbled his cards nervously, one eye on Matthew. 'Twenty.'

'That's a four, not a five!' Charlie Martin's voice was a gravelly bass. 'What's the matter with you, boy? You're like a woman with a beetle in her drawers.' He put down a ten. 'Twenty-nine.'

'Go.' Another point for Charlie.

The game came to an end, Charlie emptied his glass and signalled to the barman to refill it. Nobody expected him to move from his chair.

'I heard about your girl, Matt, a bad business, I'm sorry.' The old man had his back to Eva and he did not turn round. 'I understand that she lost her way in the fog last night and walked into the quarry.'

'That's what they are trying to say.' Matthew was surly, like a rebellious child.

'It is an easy thing to do.' When Charlie Martin was speaking seriously he enunciated each syllable very precisely, like a Highlander.

The atmosphere in the little bar was remarkable

as though everyone knew that more was being said than just the words which were spoken.

'I suppose that she was on her way back from Peters' place?'

'She had been there.'

'There must have been others, also on their way home?'

'She didn't leave at the same time. They say she left alone but . . .'

'A pity.' Charlie Martin studied his huge signet ring, twisting it round on his finger. 'That young man is not wanted in the islands.'

There was a murmur of approval.

'He murdered Sylvie.'

'That is a foolish thing to say unless you can prove it.' The old man took a sip from the tankard which the barman had set on the table by his hand. 'All the same, there can be no doubt that he has been a very bad influence on our young people.'

It was almost as though a formal resolution had been tabled and approved. Matthew Eva got up to go but Charlie, still without turning round stopped him with a raised hand. 'You will have no-one at home to cook you a meal?'

'No, but . . .'

'You will come home with me.'

At two o'clock when Sergeant Jordan wanted to speak to Matthew he had no difficulty in finding him. There were hardly any of the locals who did not know that Charlie Martin had taken him home to Sunday dinner. Jordan found them in the sitting-room of the big house under the fort. A bow window commanded an uninterrupted view of the bay, the walls were covered with photographs, mainly of ships and wrecks but some were of people dressed in the fashion of an earlier time, people, for the most part, now dead and gone.

'A drop of brandy, sergeant?' The old man and Matthew were drinking brandy out of balloon glasses.

'What I have to say to Matt is rather private, Mr Martin.'

Matthew's high colour was heightened still further by food and drink and his speech was a little slurred. 'I've nothing to hide, Freddie Jordan, what is it?'

Jordan shrugged. 'Dr Ross is unwilling to commit himself to a definite statement but he is of the opinion that Sylvie's injuries could be accounted for by the fall . . .'

Eva turned to Charlie Martin. 'What did I . . . ?'

But the old man spoke soothingly. 'Listen to the sergeant, Matt, give the man a chance.'

'According to Dr Ross, Sylvie's skull was remarkably thin and this would make her far more liable to the kind of injuries she suffered than a person with a normal skull.'

Charlie Martin nodded. 'An egg-shell skull, I came across it once – first mate on the old *Cecilia* . . . But never mind, go on, sergeant.'

'It seems that in addition to head and facial injuries she also had fractures of the left femur and tibia and a fractured pelvis.' He looked at Eva sympathetically. 'I'm sorry, Matt, but I said I would keep you informed.'

Eva was staring unseeingly at the pattern on the carpet. 'Is that all?'

'No, there's something else – two things in fact. Ross says there were no signs of sexual assault but . . .'

Eva looked up, 'But what?'

'Sylvie was four months pregnant.'

'Pregnant!' He was shocked.

'She hadn't told you?'

'Of course she hadn't told me! What sort of a damn fool do you take me for?'

Charlie swirled his brandy round the glass and sniffed. 'Had she been to see Ross?'

'A fortnight ago. She wouldn't tell him who the father was but she said she wanted to have the baby.'

'He should have told me!' Matt's chin jutted out in fresh aggression.

'He wanted to but she wouldn't let him.'

Matthew placed his glass carefully on an ornate Burmese ebony table. 'That settles it!'

Charlie Martin spoke quietly. 'Don't be stupid, Matthew, it settles nothing, it poses a question.'

'A question to which we all know the answer!' Eva rounded on the sergeant. 'Have you seen Peters?'

'I've talked to him.'

'Since you heard from Ross?'

'Yes. He says that as far as he knew Sylvie left with the others last night.'

'That's not what they say.'

'No. About the baby he said that he had no idea she was pregnant and he denied that the baby was his.'

'And you believe him?'

'I've no reason not to at the moment.'

Eva stood up, menacing. 'Are you saying . . . ?'

'The sergeant is just giving you the facts as he sees them, Matt, calm down!' Charlie Martin turned to Jordan. 'What happens next?'

Jordan was cautious. 'That will be up to the coroner and my bosses. With Dr Ross unwilling to commit himself firmly one way or the other I should think they would bring in a pathologist.'

Charlie nodded. 'Obviously the best thing, sergeant; the best thing for everybody.'

Chief Superintendent Wycliffe caught his first glimpse of the islands as the helicopter crossed the coastline of the mainland. Against the sun they appeared as low, dark silhouettes on the sea, like ships in convoy. Twenty minutes later he was looking down on the little archipelago and he was reminded of maps on the flyleaves of books about treasure voyages which he had read as a boy. Although he was now forty-six he felt the same sense of anticipation he had known as he turned over the title page and started to read at Chapter One.

It was incredibly peaceful and calm. They were flying over a small town at the end of a long, white beach. He could see boats in the harbour and people strolling along the wharf. Then they were looking down on a chequer-board of tiny fields and they had ceased to move but hovered in space like a kestrel with fluttering wings. The descent was gentle and they touched down in a field near a hut which looked like a bus station but had HELIPORT painted in big white letters on its sloping roof.

Sergeant Jordan was there, his massive form bulging in his uniform, moon-faced and slightly apprehensive. Wycliffe found it difficult to behave normally. If he had taken the four-hour sea passage it might have been easier but by this science-fiction machine the transition was too rapid, it had the quality of a magical experience. He felt as Alice must have done when she stepped through the looking glass. Jordan insisted on carrying his case.

'I've got a car outside.'

'A car?'

'It's nearly two miles.'

The air was balmy and sweet with no tang of salt, which surprised him. 'Isn't it peaceful?'

The sergeant gave him a sidelong look. 'Your first visit to the islands, sir?'

'Yes.'

'It's not always like this.'

Outside a little blue and white police car was waiting; for the other passengers on the helicopter there was a minibus. Jordan put the chief superintendent's case in the boot.

'The hotels and boarding houses are pretty full, sir, I didn't think you'd want to be with a crowd so I've fixed you up at my place – just until you have a chance to look round.'

'Thanks.'

'I hope it will suit you, sir.'

Wycliffe hoped so too.

Everything but the sea and the sky seemed to have been scaled down, tiny fields, tiny houses, roads in which it was impossible for two vehicles to pass except in a few prescribed places. They arrived on the wharf and the sergeant pulled up outside the police station. The wharf was almost deserted;

the island's fleet of boats rode at moorings, white and red and blue hulls reflected in the pale green water.

'They're having their evening meals, it'll liven up directly.' Jordan seemed anxious to forestall any possible criticism of his island but Wycliffe had still not recovered his poise.

The sergeant's house, next to the police station, fronted directly on to the wharf and his wife was waiting for them at the front door. She was a good-looking woman, with clear, smooth skin, grey hairs which she did nothing to hide and frank blue eyes which were still girlish. 'I'll show you to your room.'

His bedroom looked out on the wharf and the harbour, a bright, plainly furnished room with white walls, polished wood floor and mats. A double bed with a white, honeycomb quilt.

'I hope you haven't turned out of your room . . .'

'No, we sleep in the back, it's quieter.'

She had a meal ready by the time he had unpacked and washed, grilled mackerel with a white sauce and potatoes and carrots. When the meal was over Jordan said, 'I expect you are waiting to hear all about it.'

But Wycliffe wanted nothing more than to walk round the harbour in the gathering dusk and to drop into a pub for a beer. 'Perhaps we could go for a walk?'

'Walk? Where to?'

'Just a stroll, you could tell me what I ought to know on the way . . .'

'If you like.'

Jordan had been right; the wharf was now alive with people, people walking arm in arm or standing in little groups gossiping or sitting on the piles of timber which were stacked at intervals. The darkness was warm and soft, navigation lights on the moored craft cast ribbons of light over the water and the people in the houses along the wharf had their windows and doors open making their lives part of the life of the wharf.

'He's a keeper on the Temple Rock.'

'What?'

'Eva, the girl's father, is a keeper on the Temple Rock light. They do four weeks on and two off, he's just started his spell ashore.'

'I see.'

'He's a widower, his wife died nearly two years back and since then the girl has looked after him. She was coming up for twenty . . . It's very odd and tragic, his wife died by falling off a cliff.'

'Any suggestion of foul play there?'

'None. Poor old Matt was off on the light, it was a terrible shock for him.'

'How does . . . How did the girl manage when her father was away?'

'She stayed on in the house.'

'Alone?'

'Why not? This isn't London and there's an aunt a few doors away.'

'What sort of a girl was she? A tart?'

'By no means, she always seemed a very pleasant girl. Of course, like the rest, she got mixed up with Peters.'

'Tell me about Peters.'

Wycliffe was only half listening. A boat was coming into harbour, her red and green lights and the white light at her masthead glided between the breakwaters; he could just hear the slow throb of her engine.

'Vince Peters, I suppose you know he's the pop singer . . .'

'I've a daughter. He packed it in a year or two back, didn't he?'

'Yes, just over two years. I suppose he's made his bit and decided to pull out while the going was still good. I don't blame him but I wish he'd gone somewhere else.'

'I suppose he yearned for the simple life.'

'Don't we all? Of course the establishment here keeps a close watch on anybody trying to buy land in the islands and they wouldn't have sold Vince Peters enough to bury himself.'

'Well?'

'His lawyers worked through a front man – a respectable, retired naval officer. There were red faces when Peters turned up one morning with his guitar and his mistress.'

'Now he holds court for the island's youth – is that it?'

'You could say that.'

They had reached the Seymour Arms, the door of the saloon bar was open on to the wharf and people were sitting outside drinking. Inside it looked like a rugby scrum.

'Pity!' Wycliffe said. 'I could do with a drink.'

'I'll get it from the public. Beer for you?'

The sergeant disappeared up an alley by the pub

and returned a few minutes later with a pint in each hand. They found a seat on a pile of galvanized pipes recently unloaded from the *Islander*.

'Cheers!'

'Kids here haven't got much to amuse them. An old film on Saturday night, a youth club run by the vicar and a dance in the church hall once a month.' Jordan paused to gulp his beer and wiped his mouth. 'Peters put an old barn at their disposal, fixed them up with stereo and stacks of records and throws in, as a bonus, guitar lessons for anybody who wants them. Of course he's got them eating out of his hand.'

'No harm in that.'

'There are plenty in the islands who wouldn't agree.'

'And you?'

The sergeant watched while a young couple strolled by, absorbed in each other and mesmerised by the warm darkness. 'I don't know. Sometimes I think they're right; that he's a bad influence.'

'In what way?'

'It's difficult to pinpoint. You know what kids are, once you've got their loyalty, they can be dominated . . .'

'Do you think he killed Sylvie?'

'No. Sylvie lost her way in the fog and walked over the edge of the quarry.'

'Then why am I here?'

'With due respect, sir, that's none of my doing.'

'It's a direct result of your report to your divisional HQ. They referred it to Area and here I am.'

Jordan finished his beer. 'We islanders form a tight community.' He gestured widely with his empty tankard. 'These people, the tourists, make no real impact, life goes on apart from them . . .'

'So?'

'It doesn't take much to stir up trouble. We're like a big family, always bickering amongst ourselves but ready enough to combine against any stranger who steps out of line. With Matthew Eva shooting his mouth off about Peters it could turn ugly.'

'You mean they might take the law into their own hands?'

'It wouldn't be the first time.'

Wycliffe got out his pouch and started to fill his pipe. 'I'm not the riot squad.'

'No, but you're well known and you've no axe to grind. If, after an investigation, you say that she hasn't been murdered, they will take your word for it.'

'I'm not the coroner either.'

Jordan was unperturbed. 'All the same, I think you understand me, sir.'

Wycliffe put a match to his pipe. 'I do, too well.'

Bellings, the deputy chief, had said to him, 'It's really a diplomatic mission, Charles. The chief had a word with the Lord Warden of the Isles . . . It would be better if we at least go through the motions of an investigation into the girl's death. We don't want trouble . . .' And trouble, in the deputy chief's vocabulary, meant anything that might upset influential people. 'Look upon it as a holiday, Charles . . .' Wycliffe got up from his rather uncomfortable seat on the iron pipes. 'Dr Franks is flying over tomorrow.'

'The pathologist?'

'Yes. If we're going to play games we'll do it properly.'

Back at the Jordans' house Mrs Jordan brought in three cups of cocoa. 'I'm not very keen on cocoa,' Wycliffe said.

Mrs Jordan was brisk. 'Drink it up! It will make you sleep.'

Something did. In bed he listened for a time to footsteps on the cobbles and to snatches of conversation from people passing just below his window. A bell-buoy rocked by a slow and gentle swell clanged monotonously, then he slept.

Chapter Two

When he woke the sun was shining and the ceiling of his room was bright with dancing reflections from the waters of the harbour. His watch had stopped because he had forgotten to wind it. He got up and looked out of the window. Most of the craft in the harbour had been moved from their moorings and were lying alongside the quay. A small tanker-waggon was filling their fuel tanks by means of a long flexible hose. A very stout man in a blue jersey, with white hair and moustaches like God-the-father, seemed to be in charge. Wycliffe washed, dressed and went downstairs. It was seven o'clock but the Jordans were early risers and they were both at their breakfasts in a little kitchen at the back of the house. Jordan was like a schoolboy at the start of a holiday.

'Where do we begin, sir?'

'Begin?'

'What's the programme?'

Wycliffe looked vaguely out of the little window to the rising ground behind the house where Jordan had a vegetable patch and kept a few hens. 'I haven't got a programme.'

'Will you want to see Matthew Eva?'

'Perhaps, I don't know.'

Jordan's kindly moon-face looked hurt, he thought he had been snubbed. In fact Wycliffe had spoken the literal truth.

He was smoking his after-breakfast pipe, Mrs Jordan was washing up in their little lean-to scullery. 'Have you got a map of the islands?'

'I'll get one from the office.' He was back in a moment with an inch-to-the-mile Ordnance and spread it on the breakfast table. 'We are here.' His index finger blotted out the harbour.

'And the Peters' place?'

'Here. It's almost in the middle of the island, a quarter of a mile beyond the quarry. Salubrious Place, it's called, lying in a dip of the downs. It used to be a farm but Peters let off most of the land to a neighbouring farmer and kept the house and outbuildings.'

'I'll borrow this.' Wycliffe folded the map and slipped it into his pocket. 'Tell Mrs Jordan I'll be back for lunch.'

'What about Dr Franks?'

'He'll have to see the body and I expect he'll want to take a look at the quarry. Is there a cliff rescue team or something of that sort?'

'Of course, they're part of the volunteer service for fire and rescue in the islands.'

'Then you'd better alert them, Franks may need their help.'

'What shall I tell him, sir?'

'Tell him? Nothing, he's the expert, it's up to him to tell us.'

Jordan was disappointed in his desire to show off his island to the chief superintendent but a little flattered that he was being left to receive the pathologist.

Wycliffe stood with the sergeant at the doorway of the police station, taking in the scene. Refuelling was complete, the tanker-waggon had gone but the old man remained; he was sitting on a bollard making entries in a book with black, shiny covers.

'Who's that?'

'Charlie Martin.' The sergeant told him about Charlie Martin.

Wycliffe walked over and stood beside the old man. 'Good morning, Mr Martin.'

Charlie totted up a column of figures and entered a total. 'Good morning, Mr Wycliffe.' Evenly matched. He turned to a fresh section of the book and began another addition. Wycliffe waited.

'I suppose you know that I'm here to find out how Sylvie Eva died?'

'There will be plenty here anxious to tell you.'

'Why should Peters kill her?'

'I didn't say that he did.'

'What do you think?'

'She was pregnant.'

'That would be no reason to kill her.'

The old man shifted impatiently. 'This is not the mainland.'

'The islanders want to be rid of him, is that it?'

'We shall be glad to see him go.'

'Why?'

'Because he corrupts our young people.'

'In what way?'

The old man shrugged. He resumed his additions

and it was obvious that there was no more to be got from him.

Wycliffe climbed the hill from the town and came out on to a rough moorland, yellow with gorse. The road petered out into a track good enough for a Land-Rover, heavy going for a car. Away to his left there was an island which seemed no more than a stone's throw across the water. According to his map it was Morvyl and the channel was nearly a mile wide. There were no houses to be seen, only little square fields, green and brown, moulded to the contours of the land. Beyond Morvyl he could see the double hump of Biddock which was uninhabited and beyond Biddock, the Western Ledges with Temple Rock lighthouse rising out of the sea like a slender white finger. Calm as it was, there was a lace of foam round the base of the tower.

He followed the track for about a mile and a half until it forked. The right-hand fork was tougher and strewn with boulders but it seemed to skirt the towering granite mass of Carngluze so he followed it and came to the quarry. He stood on the lip of the quarry, looking down. The drop was sheer, a granite face with crevices from which a few tufts of sea pinks grew. At the bottom there was a shallow pool with rushes round the margin and he thought he could see the depression left by Sylvie's body.

According to his map, by continuing on his present path he would rejoin the main track not far from Salubrious Place and he would be following, in the opposite direction, the path which Sylvie must have taken to her death. In a very few minutes he was looking down into a shallow valley with a stream running through it and on the far side a copse of pines. Near the copse a stone house with outbuildings formed three sides of a courtyard, the fourth side was walled with a broad gateway, its posts surmounted by stone figures of indeterminate form. The grey slate roofs and the walls were covered with lichens and seemed to be as much part of the landscape as the granite outcrops which dotted the moor. Apart from the stream it was silent and, apparently, deserted.

Wycliffe walked down the steep track, crossed a bridge over the stream and entered the cobbled courtyard. Three or four cats lazed in the shade of an old contorted pine tree but there was no other sign of life. The house was on his left and the other two sides of the rectangle were occupied by anonymous farm buildings in a good state of repair. One of these buildings had been plastered over the stone and whitewashed providing an ideal surface for a painted inscription in letters two feet high: 'GO HOME MURDERER!' Underneath another, less expert hand, had added a sentence containing similar advice in cruder terms. Evidently the islanders had fired their opening shots.

The front door of the house stood open to a hall with stone paving partly covered by Persian rugs. He rang the doorbell and heard it jangle somewhere inside the house but nobody came. Then he heard a rhythmic thumping sound coming from one of the outhouses and made in that direction. The sound seemed to come from behind a door at the far end of the courtyard. He pushed open the door and found himself in a large whitewashed room with shelves against the wall supporting rows of greyish clay pots arranged according to shape and size. The room was L-shaped and in the angled portion a girl was working at a potter's wheel. He watched while she moulded and drew up the spinning clay into a rather elegant, round-bellied pot with a flanged rim.

'Are you looking for someone?' She continued her work.

'Mr Peters.'

'In the house.'

'I've tried but there's no answer.'

She took a wire and removed the pot from the wheel. 'Hold on.'

She was seventeen or eighteen, a pretty, plump girl with sturdy legs. Ordinary. Was she Peters' mistress? He had expected Kings Road with beads and tassels but this girl could have been doing her 'A' levels at school. She put the new pot on a shelf with others to dry.

Wycliffe introduced himself but she showed little interest. 'You've come about Sylvie?' She led him back to the house, through the hall to a large kitchen at the back where Peters was stirring something in a saucepan on the stove.

'For you, Vince. Why can't you answer the door when somebody rings?'

The kitchen window looked out across a small green meadow to the sombre pines. There was a row of beehives just short of the trees. The sun was in the front of the house and though the kitchen window was large the room seemed inadequately lit.

'Detective Chief Superintendent Wycliffe.'

Peters continued to stir whatever it was in the saucepan. The smell was appetizing.

'Mr Peters?'

'That's me.'

He was tall and very thin, round-shouldered and hollow chested but he looked younger, less dissipated than the photographs Wycliffe had seen as pin-ups and on record sleeves. The haggard, tortured look was 'in' with the kids. He had a great mop of frizzy red hair and there were carefully cultivated tufts on his cheek bones and a triangular growth on his chin but his upper lip was bare. He wore a green singlet tucked into faded blue jeans and no shoes or stockings.

'Wasn't it an accident?'

'Why do you ask?'

'Do they usually send a chief super to sort out an accident?'

'Some of the islanders are saying that she was murdered.'

'And that I murdered her?'

He held his left arm tightly against his body, slightly flexed at the elbow as though he had injured it in some way.

'Was she here on Saturday evening?'

'She was here most evenings when there was a session in the Barn. As you probably know the kids have a sort of club in the Barn.' He stopped stirring, turned down the gas and came over to the table. 'You'd better sit down.'

The kitchen had been modernized, eye-level units, laminated plastic, and old-fashioned sweet bottles, exotic with gilt labels, for stores. There was only a stool to sit on, an angular thing with chrome legs. Wycliffe perched on it uncertainly. Peters sat on the corner of the table.

'Did she always stay after the others had left?'

'No.'

'But she did on Saturday evening.'

'No.'

'The others say that she did.'

Peters shrugged.

'Did you have any conversation with her that evening?'

'We chatted for a bit.'

'What about?'

'What do people talk about?'

'Was there something special about your relationship with Sylvie – different from the others?'

'Not special – no.'

'But she was pregnant.'

'Pregnant.' Expressionless.

Wycliffe got out his pipe and started to fill it. He was trying to control his exasperation. Peters might have been in a soundproof glass box for all the communication there was between them.

'I'd like to look round.'

'Help yourself.'

'I want you to show me.'

'What?'

'The Barn for a start.'

Peters went across to the stove to see how his cooking was going, lifted the lid, sniffed and covered the saucepan once more.

'You enjoy cooking?'

'I enjoy cooking.'

'You must find life here a change from what you've been used to.'

'I get along.'

'The appeal of the simple life?'

It was like trying to scratch glass with a pencil.

As they were crossing the courtyard Wycliffe noticed that he limped. One leg – the left, dragged slightly.

Wycliffe pointed to the inscriptions. 'When were these done?'

'During the night.'

The original barn door had been remounted and had a wicket cut in it. The wood had been stripped of paint, polished and varnished to a perfect surface but the whole of the lower part of the door was blackened and blistered by a recent fire.

'This too?'

'They started a fire with shavings and paraffin.'

'You saw them?'

'It was about three in the morning; believe it or not, I was asleep.' He pointed to one of the windows. 'It was when they smashed that I woke up.'

'What did you do?'

Peters shrugged. 'We got up and put the fire out which, I suppose, was what they intended.'

'You think they smashed the window to draw your attention?

'I imagine so. They wouldn't want to burn the place down at this stage. Just a broad hint.'

'You take this very calmly, Mr Peters.'

'It's a way they have with strangers, I'm making no complaint.'

'I think you are wrong.'

'You wanted to see the Barn.'

They moved into a lofty room open to the roof trusses, cool and dimly lit. The walls were covered with evocative posters and blow-ups of pop stars, larger than life. At one end there was a platform with all the electronic gadgetry which has made the pop scene what it is and behind this, an enormous photograph of the late Jimi Hendrix in one of his orgasmic experiences with a guitar. Wycliffe was reminded of a church with its holy pictures.

'It seems that Sylvie fell into the quarry.'

Peters said nothing.

'Her skull and face were smashed in and she had a fractured pelvis and thigh.'

'Nasty!'

'Who runs the pottery?'

'It was Clarissa's idea – the girl I live with – and she runs it.'

'The girl I met when I arrived?'

'No, that's Brenda Luke, she comes in part-time to help.'

'You sell the pottery?'

'We don't give it away.'

'Where is Clarissa?'

'Gone to the farm for milk.'

'The two of you live here alone?'

'A woman comes in from the village a few hours each day.'

Wycliffe wandered round the Barn, looking at the posters, wondering what to do next. Peters watched him in silence for a while then he laughed. 'This is a fun place, man!'

'How old are you Mr Peters?'

'Twenty-eight.'

Wycliffe nodded. 'Getting beyond it.' He had the impression that Peters was uneasy, that he was putting on a not very convincing act to cover his concern.

Peters went to stand in the doorway, looking out into the courtyard. Was he sulking?

'Do you open the Barn every night?'

'Four nights a week. Mondays, Wednesdays, Saturdays and Sundays.'

'How many youngsters come each night?'

'It varies; there are between thirty and forty members and most nights about twenty turn up.'

'Only members?'

'Each member can bring a friend and during the season, like now, some of them do but not many, they like to keep it to themselves.'

'How many were here on Saturday?'

'About the usual, you can look in the book.' He turned to point to a table near the platform. 'It's in the drawer.'

The book was an ordinary club register and seemed to have been well kept. Wycliffe counted twenty-five signatures on the Saturday night, only three of whom were non-members.

'I said. The kids are exclusive.'

Turning back through the book Sylvie seemed to be one of the club's most regular attenders.

'Did Sylvie have any close friends?'

'Not that I know of.'

'What's the membership subscription?'

'There isn't one.'

'So what do you get out of it?'

'I do it for love, man.'

Ask a silly question.

'I want a list of these boys and girls.'

'Help yourself.'

Wycliffe wrote the names in his notebook.

When he had finished he came out into the still, silent courtyard drenched in blinding sunlight. The cats were lying just within the narrow strip of shade afforded by the buildings.

A girl came through the gateway carrying an enamel milk can in one hand and a basket of vegetables in the other. Wycliffe glimpsed a rather sallow face framed in straight black hair, shoulder length. She wore faded blue, bib-and-brace overalls and her figure was as slim as a boy's. She must have seen them but she gave no sign and went into the house. The cats stirred themselves, stretched and followed her.

Wycliffe puffed at his pipe, half-drugged by the sunshine and the silence. 'Clarissa – is she Italian?'

'Corsican.'

There was no point in hanging around; he had made his duty call, shown the flag. No more was required of him unless Sylvie really had been murdered except to put a stop to the islanders' schoolboy escapades. He looked at his watch. Half-past ten.

'I shall arrange for a man to keep an eye on your premises at night for the time being.'

'Suit yourself.'

Peters stood in the middle of the courtyard and watched him go. But a change had come over the ex-pop idol. It was as though the act he had put on for the superintendent had utterly exhausted him and he seemed to sag in body and spirit. Wearily, he turned and went indoors. Clarissa was in the kitchen putting away vegetables she had brought from the farm. He stood, watching her work. The unself-conscious movement of her body had always been a joy to him. Unhurried, unhesitating, never seeming to change her mind. Smooth, elegant, precise. But now he watched her with a new attention, as though seeing her about her household chores had a special significance, as though, perhaps, he did not expect to have many more opportunities.

'Police?' She continued working without looking at him.

'Yes.'

'What did he say?'

'That she was pregnant.'

'Pregnant?' She turned to face him, her dark eyes wide with surprise.

Peters sat on the corner of the table. 'I knew about it, she told me.'

She came over and stood looking up at him her small pale hands resting lightly on his thighs. 'Jackie Martin?'

He shook his head, took her face between his hands and kissed her. 'She thought that she could take your place.'

'You mean that she deliberately . . .'

'Yes.'

'Poor child!' She frowned. 'Is that why she killed herself, Vince?'

'The police think that she was murdered.'

Her dark eyes searched his face with anxious concern. 'You talked to her on Saturday?'

He nodded. 'She wanted to talk so we went for a walk. She told me about the baby and she seemed to think all she had to do was to go for the nearest parson.'

'Then?'

'Then nothing. I tried to explain but it was obviously a hell of a shock.'

Clarissa's features were set in an expression of infinite tenderness. She lifted one hand and her thin, white fingers traced the line of his arm, the arm which seemed to be immobilized against his body. His features trembled, he held her close to him with his good arm and his whole frame was shaken by deep, dry sobs. 'Help me, Clarissa!' he whispered.

Neither of them had heard Nellie Martin come in but suddenly they were aware of her standing in the doorway of the kitchen, watching, a thin little smile of contempt on her hard, lined face. She stood her ground for a moment then muttered something and a little later they could hear her moving about upstairs.

Just over the bridge Wycliffe had passed a middle-aged woman, shabbily dressed. He had wished her good morning and she had acknowledged him only by the smallest movement of her lips but when he looked back, she had stopped to stare after him. Presumably she was the Peters' daily help.

Once on the moor he made a detour back to the town, following the coastal path in its devious course round small promontories and inlets, skirting tiny coves of white sand which dazzled the eyes. He arrived back past little houses with gardens in which there were gay clumps of mesembryanthemums and tall, exotic, perennial echiums like cartoon plants from a Disney film.

Dr Franks, the pathologist, plump and chubby as an overweight baby, was waiting for him at the police station with Sergeant Jordan. In a fawn linen suit, silk shirt with a colourful cravat and sandals, the doctor looked like a rather elegant tourist of the thirties.

'You've been to the mortuary?'

'I've just come from there.'

'Well?' The two men had known each other for too long to stand on ceremony.

'Her skull bones are certainly very thin, the whole of the head is delicately structured.' Franks studied his beautifully manicured hands, the plump, pink fingers and the nails with their half-moons perfectly displayed. 'In a fall one would expect such a subject to suffer considerable bone damage.'

'The question is, did she sustain *all* her injuries in the fall?'

Franks shook his head. 'I can't answer that. I haven't seen the quarry yet. Jordan is taking me there this afternoon with a couple of chaps from the cliff-rescue service.'

'What will you be looking for?'

'From the position of the body when she was found it seems that she fell feet first with her left leg doubled under her; that would account for the pelvic and limb fractures.'

'And the rest?'

'If she died as a result of accident or if she was simply pushed over alive, they must have been inflicted by her striking the rocks as she fell.'

'And you are going to look for traces.'
'Exactly.'
'I wish you joy!'
The conversation became general. 'You've found somewhere to stay?'
'The sergeant got me in at the Atlantic, I think he had to bribe the receptionist.'
They chatted until it was time for Franks to go to his hotel for lunch. He was enthusiastic about a newly conceived project in which he planned to use the harbour as a base for cruising in the islands in his recently purchased cabin cruiser.
Wycliffe looked out at the blue untroubled waters. 'I don't suppose it's always like this.'
'Oh, we're not scared of a bit of a blow, she's a good sea boat.'
The look on Jordan's face caused Wycliffe to change the subject once more. 'There's nothing more you can tell me about the girl?'
Franks shook his head. 'Not really. It's just that the skull and facial damage seems excessive, even allowing for the fragile bone structure.'
Wycliffe lunched with the Jordans off a steak pie which was delicious but lay heavily on the stomach. At two o'clock he stood in the doorway of their little house watching the visitors crowding to the boats for the afternoon trips. Charlie Martin was there and raised his hand in enigmatic salutation. Jordan came out of the house on his way to pick up Franks. He glanced up at the cloudless blue sky, then at the scores of lightly clad trippers. 'They're going to get wet.'
'Matthew Eva – where can I find him?'
Jordan considered. 'Unless he's giving a hand on

the boats he'll most likely be at home. He lives at 6, Bethel Street, sir, it's up the alley by the Seymour Arms.'

A few minutes later Wycliffe set off along the quay in the direction of the Seymour Arms. A narrow cobbled lane ran steeply upwards past the side of the pub. Neat little houses were stepped against one another on both sides, built by men who had enough of wind and weather, earning their daily bread. A little metal sign, white letters on a blue ground, Bethel Street. The door of number six stood open. Wycliffe knocked. He was almost inside a dimly lit sitting-room which had a chiffonier, a table in the middle with a potted plant, and walls covered with photographs. A door at the other side of the room opened making a rectangle of sunlight and a thickset man in a seaman's jersey came forward to meet him.

'Mr Eva?'

'That's me.'

'Wycliffe. Detective Chief Superintendent.'

'I know.' His manner was distant but not aggressive. 'You'd better come in.'

They went through the dismal little sitting-room which was probably never used into a bright, tidy kitchen with a shiny electric cooker and a large plastic-topped table on which there were the remnants of a meal.

'I just finished my dinner.' Eva gestured vaguely at the dirty dishes. 'Not had time to clear away.'

Otherwise the place was meticulously clean and orderly like a well-run ship's galley. Outside the window a yard, a little garden beyond with fruit trees and a few greens.

Wycliffe offered his sympathy. Eva got out his tobacco pouch and pushed it over. 'Smoke?' Wycliffe started to fill his pipe.

'I'll miss her, there's no denying that.'

'You are a widower?'

'Two years. Sylvie kept house since then. A good girl. I'm a keeper on the Temple Light – away a month at a time and she looked after the place . . .' The blue eyes glistened.

'You think that she was murdered?'

'I know she was, mister, no two ways about that!' His aggression flared, but he controlled it. He took back his pouch and started to fill his own pipe. 'Sylvie knew this island like the back of her hand. Since she was old enough to go out by herself she's wandered over it till she got to know it better than I do myself.' He paused in the act of pressing down the tobacco in his pipe to look Wycliffe straight in the eyes. 'She *couldn't* have lost herself!'

'I understand that there was a dense fog . . .'

'Fog? It was no more than a bit of mist then but even if she'd been blindfold she couldn't have walked into that quarry by no accident.'

'What if she did it on purpose?'

'You mean suicide?'

'It's possible.' Wycliffe looked at the shining window panes, the bright paintwork and the polished linoleum to remind himself that he was talking about a real person, a girl who would have made a good wife and mother and would probably have known as much happiness as most. 'She was pregnant; even in these days there are still girls who can't bring themselves to face . . .'

Eva nodded. 'I know what you're getting at. It's true Sylvie was strictly brought up according to how things are these days but if she wanted to do away with herself she wouldn't have done it that way.'

Wycliffe spoke gently. 'Why not?'

'I tell you she wouldn't!' He almost shouted.

Wycliffe smoked in silence. A cat leapt on to the window ledge outside and Eva went to open the door.

'It was the way her mother went.'

'Suicide?' Wycliffe was taken off-guard.

'No!' Eva was like a rumbling volcano, ready at any moment to erupt into violence but who could blame him? 'They were out for a walk along the cliffs – like sisters they was rather than mother and daughter. It was rough, blowing a gale – October. Sylvie turned to speak to her mother and she wasn't there . . . They found her that evening. I was on the rock and it was three days before they could get a boat off to fetch me.'

'What a terrible thing for both of you!'

Eva sat stroking the blond hairs on his wrist. 'She took it bad. For a week she scarcely spoke but she come to terms in the end like we all have to.'

The cat, a magnificent black and white tom, was mewing plaintively and rubbing round the table leg. Eva got up to pour milk into a saucer on the floor.

'I suppose Sylvie had boy friends?'

Eva looked up angrily but changed his mind. 'At the time her mother died she was going out with a young man. Jackie Martin, he's a year or two older than Sylvie but none the worse for that. He's an island boy – been away to college and come back to teach in the school.'

'Any relation to Charlie Martin?'

Eva laughed shortly. 'All the Martins are related. Originally there was really only three families in the islands, the Martins, the Jordans and the Evas but we don't take much count of relationships beyond second cousins.' He paused to collect his thoughts. 'Anyway, as I was saying, they took up together and her mother and me was content. He wasn't what we would have chosen for Sylvie but he seemed a quiet, decent lad and one of us.' He smoked in silence for a while. 'Mother's boy – that's his trouble but it takes all sorts. I thought that as soon as Sylvie got over the first shock the two of them would have made a match of it. But it wasn't to be . . .'

Eva was staring at his cat who had finished the milk and was now stretched out on the mat in a patch of sunlight, washing himself. 'By the time she got round to going out again Peters had opened his club and all the youngsters was off there every chance. She went there a few times with Jackie but it wasn't his style – nor mine from what I hear.'

'What do you hear?'

He shrugged angrily. 'It's easy to see what he gets out of it! Anyway, I told Sylvie she wasn't to go there but what can you do with a girl of nearly twenty?' He gestured helplessly with his large hands.

'When I came home on my next shore leave I could see that it was all over between her and Jackie. She was off to Peters' place most every night and there was nothing I could do to stop it. I must admit it took her out of herself a bit but I didn't like it – not one bit!'

'When did you come home on your present leave, Mr Eva?'

He had to think, time had acquired a different meaning for him recently. 'Thursday – Thursday afternoon, it must have been.'

'Did you notice any change in Sylvie?'

He hesitated. 'Yes I did. She seemed excited – full of something.'

'Happy?'

'Not happy exactly.'

'Worried?'

'Not worried either – just excited, keyed up. I must admit I didn't think much about it, you know what girls are. I asked her if there was anything up and she pretended not to know what I was talking about – said she was no different to usual, that it was my imagination.'

Wycliffe smoked, staring out of the window at the blackcurrant bushes. The sky was no longer blue, it was smoky-grey and he remembered Sergeant Jordan's prophecy – 'They'll get wet.'

'It looks as though it's going to rain.'

Eva did not bother to look out of the window. 'Aye.'

Without being aware of when the change had taken place Wycliffe realized that he no longer thought of the investigation as a sham. He was thinking and behaving as though Sylvie's death had not been an accident.

The sky was darkening rapidly and the kitchen, which a few minutes earlier had been full of sunshine, was dimly lit as though with the approach of night.

'Storm coming up?'

'The glass has been dropping since first thing this morning but it won't last long.'

'I would like to take a look at Sylvie's room.'

Eva nodded and led the way up steep, narrow stairs to a tiny landing off which two doors opened. 'There's only two bedrooms, this is Sylvie's.'

It was a small room with a sloping ceiling and a dormer window overlooking the back garden. The walls were white and the divan bed had a white quilt. There was a tiny wardrobe, a chest of drawers and a table under the window with a record player on it and a small stack of records. On the chest of drawers, apart from a swing mirror and a few toilet articles there was a framed photograph of a grave faced, attractive woman of about forty.

'My wife,' Eva said from the landing.

Wycliffe made a vague gesture at the drawers. 'Have you . . . ?'

Eva shook his head dumbly. The drawers were lined with white paper and scrupulously tidy. One contained her underclothes, one was full of back numbers of a girl's magazine. One of the two top drawers had in it a couple of handbags, three or four belts and a box with a few bits of cheap jewellery. Eva was watching him. 'It's not much, is it?' Wycliffe knew what he meant.

The other top drawer held handkerchiefs and scarves but underneath them there were two albums and a diary. One of the albums contained family photographs with Sylvie herself figuring in most of them at all stages of her growing up. The other album was a scrap book devoted exclusively to Vince Peters.

There were pictures and clippings from newspapers but there were also originals which he must have given her and, in pride of place, a studio portrait of him inscribed: 'To Sylvie with love from Vince 1971.' The diary had most of its pages blank but from time to time there were cryptic entries usually involving initials. On the 15th April she had written in bold print '280 days!' and on the 20th July there was an entry 'It's definite'.

'I'm afraid that I shall have to send someone to make a proper search.'

Eva shrugged and said nothing.

'I'll be seeing you again, Mr Eva, meantime . . .'

Eva saw him to the door and stood watching as he hurried down the cobbled alley to the quay. As he reached the quay fat raindrops were beginning to fall out of a leaden sky making large, circular wet patches on the tarmac.

Chapter Three

The worst of the rain had spent itself within the hour but the wind which sprang up behind it blew steadily, raising a choppy sea and giving the trippers a bonus thrill. The boats returned early, while it was still raining, and Wycliffe, standing in the front room of Jordan's house, watched the passengers coming ashore, wet but cheerful, with spray on their faces and the tang of salt on their lips. Charlie Martin was there, standing aloof but with an eye for everything. In his oilskins and sou'wester he seemed as indifferent to the weather as the Temple Rock itself.

It was after six when Sergeant Jordan returned with Franks. Fortunately Jordan had insisted on them being prepared for rain and they were none the worse.

'I managed to get a good look at the face before the rain came.' The tubby little doctor was pleased with himself, having shown the cliff-rescue people that he could make good use of a bo'sun's chair. 'There are no signs I can find that she hit the rock on the way down. The face isn't as sheer or as smooth as it looks, there are bosses and ridges where a falling body might strike but I don't think she did. As far as I can tell she fell clear.'

They were sitting in Jordan's front room, drinking

tea out of willow-patterned cups. Franks added a second spoonful of sugar to his tea and stirred absently.

'So?' Wycliffe was impatient.

The doctor considered his words. He liked to make a good story. 'In my opinion she fell feet first and her landing was responsible for the fractured limb bones and pelvis.'

'What about the damage to her skull?'

Franks was staring out of the little window at people passing by. 'I don't see how that could have been caused by the fall.'

'But the head injuries killed her?'

'Without doubt.'

'So it's murder.'

'She obviously didn't do it herself.'

Wycliffe got out his pipe and started to fill it. 'Presumably she was attacked, battered about the head, then her body was pushed into the quarry.'

Franks nodded. 'That would fit the facts as I know them.'

'What about the weapon?'

'Weapon?'

'Whoever did it couldn't have used his bare hands.'

Franks ran his fingers through thinning hair. 'As usual, you want me to do your job for you. The very extent of the injuries makes it difficult to come to any conclusion about the nature of the weapon but if I must say something, it's this – with her skull the weapon need not have been heavy or the blow powerful. It's really quite remarkable that she got through her life so far without some sort of skull fracture. A severe bump on the head would have been enough, the sort most kids get some time or other.'

'How many blows – two, three – many?'

Franks grinned. 'Your confidence is touching. The answer is that I don't know. I should have thought more than one blow from a weapon with a relatively small surface but a single blow from a weapon with a large surface of contact would have been enough.'

Before his evening meal Wycliffe spoke on the telephone with Chief Inspector Gill, his Number Two at the Crime Squad.

'You want me to come over?'

'Yes, get the first flight in the morning.'

'What's the weather like?'

'Don't bother with your suntan lotion.'

'We can call on divisional assistance as we need it but you'd better bring a team – who's free?'

Arrangements made, Wycliffe had his meal. Sergeant Jordan was subdued and Wycliffe preoccupied. 'We shall need a headquarters. In view of the accommodation problem we shall have to make arrangements for our chaps to sleep and eat there. A church hall – something of the sort.'

'The school is shut for the holidays, there's a canteen . . .'

'Good! See what you can do.'

'I'll see the headmaster in the morning.'

'Tonight.' Wycliffe was a changed man, gone was the rather sleepy benevolence which had puzzled the sergeant.

All the same, after his meal and while Jordan was trying to get authority to use the school as a headquarters, Wycliffe was on his way to the Seymour Arms. There were not many people about, partly because it was the time of the evening meal in hotels and boarding houses, but also because the strong wind was sweeping rain squalls across the island. Overhead smoky clouds chased each other and above them the sky was dun coloured giving no sign of where the sun might be. Wycliffe turned up the collar of his coat and kept close in under the houses.

There were few customers in the public bar of the Seymour. Charlie Martin was in his usual place, reading a newspaper. Three men were playing darts. The landlord, not yet needed in the saloon, had been chatting to Martin. His attitude to Wycliffe was civil but distant. Wycliffe took his drink to a seat near the bar from where he had a good view of the whole room. Charlie, after a curt nod, went back to his newspaper. For the darts players it seemed that Wycliffe did not exist.

One of them was dark and stocky with a red face and a big paunch from too much beer-drinking. His appearance was not improved by a cast in his sight. The second man was taller and in better shape; he was fair, with sideboards and tracts of hair across his cheeks which linked with a luxuriant, silky moustache. The third man was older and very tall. His face was fleshy with thick lips, he had a stubbly beard and spiky white hair. Wycliffe was struck by his eyes which, when they were not focused on anything in particular, had a wild look, like the eyes of an animal. The others seemed to humour him and they paid for his drinks.

More customers arrived, ordered their drinks and disposed themselves round the room, taking seats which through long usage they had come to regard as their own. Nobody seemed to notice Wycliffe. Four of the men settled down to a game of whist while two others got out a chequer-board. They were following a well-established routine and there was no need to say much. Wycliffe sipped his drink and watched. A pall of blue smoke grew and floated just below the raftered ceiling.

The darts game finished and the players came over to the bar to replenish their glasses. The man with the red face turned to Wycliffe.

'Was she murdered or wasn't she?'

'It seems very likely that she was.'

The red-faced man opened his mouth to say something but Charlie Martin cut in. 'Will you be making an arrest?'

Wycliffe shook his head. 'It's far too early to be talking about an arrest. To do that we need evidence – evidence pointing to a single person.'

There was a derisory laugh from the company and the old man frowned. 'But there will be a full police inquiry?'

'Of course.'

'Good!' After taking a mouthful of beer and carefully wiping his moustache with a red and white pocket handkerchief, he got up, went to a wall cupboard and came back with a cribbage board and a pack of cards. 'You will play a game with me, Mr Wycliffe?' It was the accolade of acceptance. Everybody in the bar was paying attention.

'I'm sorry, cribbage is not one of my games.'

'Pity!' Martin looked round the room in the manner of an officer choosing a subordinate for a mission. 'Henry! Give me a game if you please.'

A middle-aged, black-bearded man in a reefer jacket with brass buttons, joined the old man at his table. 'Our harbour master, Mr Wycliffe – Captain Osborne.' Wycliffe acknowledged the introduction and the two men settled to their play.

Wycliffe was disappointed, he had hoped that the atmosphere of the bar would have loosened tongues but it seemed that they all took their cue from the old man.

The darts players were still standing at the bar and one of them, the white-haired chap with the thick lips, caught Wycliffe's eye and gave a significant jerk of his head in the direction of the door. A few minutes later he drank up his beer and left. Wycliffe waited for a while, then, after a word with Charlie Martin and the harbour master, he followed.

The quay was almost deserted. A hardy couple, determined to make the most of their holiday, plodded along heads down to the wind, but there was no-one else in sight. Beyond the breakwater there were white flecks on the sea and in the harbour smaller craft tossed uneasily at their moorings. It was a very different scene from the one which had greeted him on his arrival when Jordan had said, 'It's not always like this.'

As he was passing the boatmen's shelter his name was called and he turned to see the white-haired man with the wild eyes standing in the doorway.

He followed him into the little hut which was just big enough for a table with a bench on either side.

There was a strong smell of paraffin but it was cosy enough; the whitewashed stone must have seen generations of fishermen come and go before tourists set foot in the island.

'You said you wanted evidence.' The man towered over Wycliffe. His manner was both aggressive and nervous; he shifted from one foot to the other and darted quick glances round the hut, almost as though he were looking for a way of escape.

'Who are you?'

'Marsden – Nick Marsden. I just wanted to . . .'

'Where do you live?'

'Quincey Cove – down the valley from Peters' place.'

'Well?'

'I was on me way home and I saw him . . .'

'Who?'

'Peters.'

'When was this?'

'The night he knocked off Sylvie Eva. He was with her.'

'Where?'

'I saw 'em come out of his place together.'

'Where did they go? What direction?'

'Up the valley. They walked up the valley by the stream.'

'Towards the farm?'

He nodded. 'They was falling out.'

'What about?'

He shook his head vaguely and the wild look came into his eyes. 'I couldn't hear what they was saying.'

'But you knew they were quarrelling.'

'Yes, I knew, you could tell.'
'Did you follow them?'
A sheepish look. 'A bit.'
'Where did they go?'
'They must've gone to the quarry.' Sly.
'By following the stream? Don't try to be clever. You stopped following them – why?'
'He's a bastard.'
'But why did you stop following them?'
'He turned round and saw me.'
'Well?'
'He told me to bugger off.' He passed his hand over his head where the hair stood up in white bristles like a clothes brush. 'He was real mad at her – shouting.'
Marsden was not drunk but he had had enough to drink. His thick lips were moist and he breathed through them making a sort of bubbling noise as he did so.
'What have you got against Peters?'
'He's a bastard.'
'You said. But what have you got against him?'
'He killed Sylvie, didn't he?' An aggressive thrust of the stubbly chin.
'Remember that it's a very serious offence to try to mislead the police in a murder inquiry.'
'I ain't misleading you, I only told you what I saw.'
'All right! If you are of the same mind in the morning you can come to my headquarters and make a statement.' Wycliffe turned to go.
'Bloody coppers!'
'By the way, why couldn't you have told me this in the pub?'

Marsden looked aggrieved. 'Well I couldn't could I? That was Peters' brother I was with.'

'The chap with a moustache?'

'Aye.'

Wycliffe stepped out on to the quay and Marsden followed him. After a few yards Wycliffe looked round, Marsden was padding back to the Seymour.

Now that he seemed to have a case to work on Wycliffe was anxious to get started; he chafed at the inevitable delay before he would have a headquarters properly organized and his men deployed. Chief Inspector Gill would be the driving force and he could not arrive in the islands for another twelve hours. It was impossible to sit still and wait. The rain had gone, the wind had dropped and the sky was clearing. Away to the west broken clouds were reddened by the setting sun.

He decided that he would take another look at Salubrious Place; at least he would find out whether Sylvie's death had put a stop to the nightly sessions there. He climbed the hill out of the town and came up on to the moor in gathering darkness. The beam of Temple Rock light swept the sky every twenty seconds, dimmed by the rapidly fading twilight. On this, his second trip, it seemed a much shorter distance to the point where he could look down into the valley. There were lights in the house and in the outbuildings but what caught and held him was the fountain of sound which seemed to well up out of the valley: raucous, metallic and underscored by a powerful, throbbing pulse which could be felt rather than heard. It was uncanny in this deserted place. He descended the steep stony track, crossed the bridge and entered the courtyard.

The single window of the Barn cast a rectangular kaleidoscopic pattern of flickering and flashing colours on the cobbles. Evidently they had all the psychedelic props. Wycliffe stood at the window and looked in. Under the darting, dancing and stabbing lights ten or a dozen couples gyrated, writhed, wriggled and jerked in serpentine ecstasy to the monstrous rhythm of drums and guitars, amplified to the level of stupefaction.

Near the window a girl with small, pale features, wearing a red, sheath mini-dress, danced with closed eyes, lost to everything but the rhythm, even to her pimply-faced partner. Peters was there, wearing black tight trousers and a black turtle-necked sweater. He was not dancing but moving slowly among the dancers, watching. They seemed unaware of him – unaware of everything but the rhythm. The foreign girl – Clarissa – was there also, dancing opposite a hefty blond youth with a broken nose. Wycliffe went inside and stood at the end of the hall waiting for a break in the barrage of sound. It came at last; abruptly, without warning, so that the senses reeled under the impact of silence. The couples stopped dancing, seemed to emerge briskly from their trances and began to chatter. Peters came over to the chief superintendent with a sardonic grin on his face but his eyes were grave.

'Come to dance, man?'

Wycliffe was grim. 'Sylvie Eva was murdered.'

'Well! That really is a drag, man.' If Peters was putting on an act to incense Wycliffe he succeeded.

Wycliffe wandered round the hall feeling slightly

ridiculous, expecting to see derisive grins, but modern youth are so practised in the acceptance of the bizarre that a middle-aged detective invading their private stamping ground is unlikely to cause the turning of a single head.

'Were you here on Saturday evening?'

'Me?' The youth addressed, pimply and inoffensive, looked surprised.

'Yes, you!' Wycliffe was unnecessarily brusque.

'Saturday? Yes, I was here.'

'What time did you leave?'

The youth shrugged. 'Half-eleven, give or take five minutes.'

'With the others?'

'Yeh – we went together as always.'

'But not with Sylvie Eva?'

'I can't hear you.'

The comparative silence had been split apart by a banshee howl as a canned singer launched into his number.

'Let's go outside,' Wycliffe suggested.

The young man looked across at a mousey little girl in jeans and a suede jacket who stood watching them. 'It's Georgina – she's my girl.'

'Then bring her with you.'

Outside in the courtyard it was fresh, the air clean and sharp with the tang of the sea.

'What's your name?'

'Nance – Jeremy Nance.'

'And yours?'

'Georgina Keys.'

'How old are you?'

'Sixteen – both of us.'

'You enjoy coming here?'

The boy was enthusiastic. 'It's great, isn't it, Georgie?'

'Yeh – great!' She was plain and skinny, her features were a little pinched but the boy seemed to defer to her in everything.

They moved over to the metal chairs under the pine tree and sat down; it was chilly but it was possible to talk. The mood had changed in the Barn and somebody with an engaging, throaty baritone voice was singing to a guitar accompaniment—

'Hear the news and the weather
Though they're always the same;
Read the cereal packet
For the novelty game;
Then have a go at a crossword
Till you're stuck for a clue;
And while you think you're killing time,
It's time that's killing you,
It's time that's killing you.'

'That's Vince – isn't he great?'

Georgie listened, entranced. 'That's special, we can't get him to sing very often . . . Isn't he super?'

'On Saturday night Sylvie did not leave at the same time as the rest of you?'

'What? – Oh, no, she didn't.'

'Did she usually go home with you?'

'Sometimes she stayed on.'

'Why?'

It was light enough to see the boy's embarrassed

shrug. Georgie had no such inhibitions. 'She had a thing about Vince, she was always round his neck.'
'Did she go to bed with him?'
'What do you think?'
'Was Peters specially keen on Sylvie?'
The girl laughed. 'You must be joking! Vince can always take or leave it and as for Sylvie, I know she's dead but let's face it, she was a bit of a drag.'
'Oh, I wouldn't say that; Sylvie was OK.' Jerry tried to be fair.
'Didn't she come with a boy friend?'
'She came sometimes with Jackie Martin, the schoolteacher, but that was a while ago. He stopped coming, I think he was too old,' Jerry said.
'I don't know about that, Sylvie was quite old – anyway she stopped bringing him and she hasn't come with anybody else. Jackie Martin still hung around to take her home some nights.'
'And Sylvie got mad about it.'
Georgie sneered. 'Sylvie pretended to get mad.'
Peters' voice came over again, they must have been dancing in between—

'Watch some more television
Like the evening before;
Test your wit and your knowledge,
Disagree with the score,
So go to bed with a novel
To find out what real lovers do:
    And while you think you're killing time,
    It's time that's killing you,
    It's time that's killing you.'

'Tell me about Saturday night – when did you first miss Sylvie?'

'Got a ciggie, Jerry?'

The boy handed her a packet of cigarettes and a box of matches. 'We didn't *miss* her like that, she just wasn't with us on the way home.'

'Nobody mentioned the fact?'

Georgie fumbled with her cigarette, choking on the smoke. 'One of the girls said something about it being Sylvie's turn.'

'Her turn?'

'With Vince, some of the girls get a kick out of him.'

'Not Georgie, we're going steady, aren't we, Georgie?'

'That's what you say.' She pulled her skimpy suede jacket more tightly round her and shivered. 'It's cold!'

'I won't keep you long. Was it foggy?'

'A bit, not bad; you could see all right.'

'I think it got worse later.'

'Do you know Nick Marsden?'

Georgie giggled. 'Nick? He's crackers.'

'He spies on us,' the boy said, 'but nobody takes any notice of him.'

'Did Sylvie have girl friends?'

Georgie hesitated. 'She didn't have many friends: her only special friend was Sally Rowse.'

'Is Sally here tonight?'

'No, I don't think her mother would let her come.'

Wycliffe stood up. 'Well, thank you both for your help. I may want you to make a statement tomorrow.'

'Did somebody kill Sylvie?'

'We've got to find out.'

Peters was ending his song—

'Don't see people but shadows
Don't have wishes but dreams
Don't know things but their pictures
Not what is but what seems;
Rather have a stained-glass window
Than one you can really see through;
    And while you think you're killing time,
    It's time that's killing you,
    It's time that's killing you.'

The applause was flattering.

'We'll get back, he might do an encore.'

Two things occurred to him. One was that despite the fuss they were making few of the islanders really believed that Sylvie had been murdered. Had they believed it there would not have been a score of youngsters at the Peters' place two nights later. The other was that the youth of the island had a good deal in common with their mainland brothers and sisters.

The two youngsters had gone back inside but Wycliffe lit his pipe and strolled round the courtyard, smoking. The clouds had gone and the indigo sky was full of stars; the mood in the Barn had changed too, beat and protest had given place to ballads, sentimental and easier on the eardrums. During the quieter passages he thought that he could hear the surf on the beaches though the nearest sea must have been more than a mile away.

Sylvie Eva had been murdered; Sylvie Eva had

been pregnant. The two facts might have been added up quite simply once, but not now, not even on the island. But, on the face of it, it seemed that Peters had gone in for murder. What motive could he have had? Passion? Not with half the girls on the island anxious to jump into bed with him. Fear? Of what? Wycliffe shrugged, it was too soon to look for conclusions.

At last the music stopped, the flashing lights were switched off and the youngsters started to leave. ' 'Night, Vince . . . 'Night, Clarissa . . . See you Wednesday . . .' All very conventional and respectable. A few minutes after they had gone Clarissa came out and crossed the courtyard with a light, quick step. Lights sprang up in the house. He could still hear voices and laughter from the other side of the valley as the kids made their way home. They were not oppressed by Sylvie's death. When Peters came out Wycliffe intercepted him.

'I would like a word with you, Mr Peters.'

'Still here, superintendent? The night is young – come in.'

'You may not want Miss . . .'

'Clarissa and I have no secrets.'

He was shown into a large sitting-room at the back of the house. One wall was made up of floor to ceiling curtains, presumably because the stonework had been replaced by glass. The room had been furnished out of the modern-furnishings department of Harrods and it looked like a studio set for a stock-broker's drawing-room. Peters seemed older, more serious, worried. Perhaps he was tired.

Wycliffe had to sit on a monstrous black leather settee.

'Drink? Whisky? Vodka? Gin?'

'Whisky.'

'Does that mean that I'm not suspected?'

'It means that I can do with a drink.'

The walls were painted dove grey, and there were several modern paintings on plinths. Wycliffe recognized a Piper and two Bratbys. Peters poured out whisky for Wycliffe and orange juice for himself.

'Here's to the Scene!'

'I am told that you were having an affair with the dead girl.'

Peters grinned. 'Is that what they say?'

'And with several of the other girls who come here.'

'It's not illegal, is it?'

'Not if the girls are over the age of consent.'

Peters was silky. 'I'm always very careful about that.'

'Giving the local dollies a treat – is that the angle?'

Peters was reproving. 'That's not quite nice, Mr Wycliffe.'

'It's a hazardous game in a place like this.'

'But it was not I who was murdered.'

The door opened and Clarissa came in carrying a tray with two steaming pottery mugs on it. She had changed into a black, silk trouser suit which clung to her body. She was obviously surprised to find Wycliffe there. 'I'm sorry, Vince, I did not know . . . I made the cocoa . . .' She spoke with clipped precision.

Wycliffe had difficulty in covering his amusement.

It must mean something that Vince Peters, ex-pop idol and notorious sex symbol, went to bed on cocoa.

Clarissa put the tray down on a low table and looked questioningly at Peters.

'Ma'moiselle Loiseau, Detective Chief Superintendent Wycliffe.' Peters made the introductions with a flourish. 'Mr Wycliffe thinks that I murdered Sylvie.'

'That is foolish!' The dark eyes rested on Wycliffe in quick appraisal. She was small, fragile, exquisite, an exhibition piece too precious one might think for everyday use, but there was strength in the set of her jaw and fire in her eye.

'Somebody killed her,' Wycliffe said. 'Somebody beat her over the head and face then pushed her body into the quarry.'

'That is terrible but it was not Vince – he could not harm anybody. I know what the islanders say and sometimes he is foolish but . . .'

'. . . underneath there beats a heart of gold. The superintendent doesn't believe it.'

Wycliffe sipped his whisky. 'You told me this morning that Sylvie had no close friends . . .'

'I told you that I didn't know of any.'

'But what about Jackie?' Clarissa pronounced the name in two quite distinct syllables.

'The schoolteacher?' Wycliffe asked. 'I thought that had been broken off . . .'

'It has.'

'Pooh! A lovers' . . . How do you say? A small quarrel. When he is here he talks to me – I can tell. He is in love, that boy.'

'He comes here?'

'But certainly! Not to the Barn, you understand, that he does not like, but he is a friend of Vince . . .'

Peters was not pleased. 'He comes here to see me because we are both interested in the same thing.'

'And what is that?'

'Flies!' To Clarissa it was obviously an inconceivable preoccupation. 'They are – how do you say – Dipters – is that right?'

'Dipterists.'

'Yes, they collect flies!' She squirmed deliciously. 'Vince does not like me to tell people.'

'Which doesn't stop you.'

Wycliffe noted that since they had come into the house Peters had not once addressed him as 'man'.

'You also told me that Sylvie did not stay behind on Saturday night after the others had gone.'

'That's right, she didn't.'

'No, she did not! Sometimes . . . but not on Saturday; on Saturday it was just like now, the two of us.'

'The other youngsters say that she was not with them.'

'I can't say about that.' Peters sipped his cocoa.

'A witness states that you were seen with Sylvie Eva walking in the direction of the farm.'

'What witness? As you must know by now some of the islanders would say anything they thought would shop me.'

Wycliffe was content not to press the point for the moment. Softly walkee . . . 'You will be required to make a statement, Mr Peters.'

'Any time.'

Wycliffe walked home in the starlight. Not far

from Salubrious Place he met Nick Marsden shambling along the track, on his way home. He was too far gone to bother with Wycliffe.

Jordan was waiting up for him, the clock on the mantelshelf showed half an hour after midnight and Jordan was mildly reproachful, 'Mr Bellings, the deputy chief has been trying to get you on the telephone, sir.'

'I don't doubt it.'

'And several newspapers . . .'

'What about the school?'

'That's fixed. The chairman of the Education Committee was on to me earlier; apparently Chief Inspector Gill telephoned him direct.'

'Good old Jimmy!' Wycliffe was glad that he would be seeing him in the morning. 'Anything else?'

'Dr Franks left a message for you to ring him at his hotel.' Jordan consulted a scrap of paper. 'The number is 221.'

Franks answered from his bed. 'I'd given you up.' He sounded weary. 'I'll send you my report but I tell you now there will be very little new in it. I'm satisfied that her injuries cannot be wholly attributed to the fall. The skull damage must have been inflicted before her body was pushed into the quarry and it was the skull damage which killed her.'

'Anything more on the weapon?'

Franks seemed to hesitate. 'Next to nothing, I searched the wounds very thoroughly for foreign matter.'

'Well?'

'I found a few fragments of rust – tiny red flakes.'

'An iron bar of some sort.'

'It looks like it. Not the sort of thing your well-dressed gent carried about with him.'

'No, but there's plenty of scrap lying about out there.' Wycliffe considered. 'It would be worth a search, he's not likely to have taken the thing home with him.'

'The trouble will be to recognize it when you find it.'

'You confirmed the pregnancy?'

'No doubt about that.'

'Blood groups?'

'The mother was group O and the baby A.'

Wycliffe made a considerable effort of recollection. 'So the father must be group A or AB – is that right?'

'Quite right.'

'Thanks, it's better than nothing.'

'Our motto is service.'

'Good night.'

Wycliffe was thoughtful. The investigation had started to silence local gossip but it was now certain that the gossip had been well founded. Sylvie had been murdered and that is what had been claimed. Now, looking for a number one suspect, who filled the bill but Peters? And they had said that too.

Wycliffe believed that, over the years, he had acquired the ability to exclude at will, certain topics from his mind. If he worried about his cases at all it was at the subconscious level or because he chose to worry in the hope that some constructive idea might emerge. Now he went to bed and to sleep, dreaming that he was on a rocky shore facing an incoming tide with a wall of high cliffs behind him. Only when the water was lapping round his ankles and he was clawing at the smooth rock face with his fingers, did he wake, his heart racing, his nails digging into his palms.

Vince Peters lay awake far into the night but that was nothing new. He had sleeping tablets but his doctor had told him that his insomnia was voluntary. Which was true, up to a point. He was greedy for life, each night he was reluctant to snap the last thin thread of consciousness. In any case he liked to take stock of himself, to strike a balance for the day. This morning he had had pins and needles in his left leg. But there seemed to be some easing of the rigidity in his arm . . . And what about his mind? Who could tell?

Sometimes he could look at himself objectively, as a case for treatment. But for him there was no treatment. It came on like the tide, advancing, retreating and again advancing, gaining a little each time.

Then there was the business of the girl. He felt sorry for her, poor little cow. But one way and another she had been asking for it. The doe-eyed copper had seemed suspicious and he and his mates would probably ferret out the truth in the end. Bully for them! Why should he care? But he did. He thought of Jackie Martin and grinned to himself. Probably Jackie had made his statement to the police already and wet his trousers in the process.

He sighed and turned over. Clarissa stirred in her sleep.

Chapter Four

Next day the routine of a murder investigation was getting under way. Chief Inspector Gill arrived with four crime squad detectives and a uniformed sergeant with three constables from Division. They moved into the school, a fairly new building, glass and concrete with shiny parquet floors on which it was difficult to stand up. Two classrooms became dormitories with beds and blankets supplied by the island's emergency service. The headmaster's office became Wycliffe's and Gill was given the office of the deputy head. A telephone engineer was busy draping temporary cables round the building to provide extra telephones and a switchboard was set up in the main hall which was to be the control room. A police radio mechanic was installing a two-way radio-control panel to handle messages through the personal radios of the men and in the canteen two local women were preparing meals.

Wycliffe brought Chief Inspector Gill up to date on the case then he wandered round the school getting the feel of it, like a dog in a new home. Gill sat on a table in the hall, directing operations and smoking his black cheroots. Already three detectives were taking statements from the young people who had been at the Barn on Saturday night. Jeremy

Nance was there with his girl friend, looking very important. Nick Marsden was there, sitting on a form by himself looking lost.

Finally Wycliffe seated himself behind the headmaster's desk and, almost immediately, Jimmy Gill came in with a small sheaf of typescript – the first reports. He looked round the office and his ugly, rubbery face wrinkled expressively.

'Schools give me the creeps.'

'You've got a guilty conscience, my lad!'

Gill slid the papers into Wycliffe's tray.

'Anything there?'

'This might interest you.' Gill extracted a typewritten sheet from the pile and started to quote from it. 'Vincent Steven Peters, born 22nd April 1944 . . . 4 Mill Lane, Bolton, Lancs . . . Educated Falls Road Junior, Bolton Grammar and Birmingham University . . . He didn't stay the course – packed in at the end of the first year to join a folk group called The Mariners. Later they went in for pop and changed their name to The Sockets. During a European tour with the group in 1970 he met Clarissa Loisseau, a Corsican girl who was living in Paris. They lived together and continued to do so after he left the group.'

'I suppose it would have been bad for his image to get married. Anything else?'

'Only that when he left The Sockets it's estimated that he must have been worth half-a-million.'

'Anything from CRO?'

'Nothing against him.'

Wycliffe sighed. 'It's a funny world.'

'More peculiar than funny, I'd say,' Gill remarked.

'Any news of the inquest?'

'It's fixed for this afternoon. The coroner will take evidence of identification and adjourn. Jordan will be there, of course.'

'You'd better go.'

Wycliffe told him what little Franks had been able to discover about the weapon. 'It's worth a try, Jimmy. Get some men out there and search. After all there can't be all that many bits of iron lying around which are easily portable and suitable as a weapon.'

'Needles in haystacks are our speciality,' Gill said.

Very little emerged from the morning's work. One of the girls said that far from staying on after the others, Sylvie had left early on the night she died. Wycliffe spoke to the girl himself. A tall, well-made teenager with blonde hair to her shoulders, straight and sleek as a waterfall.

'You are Sally Rowse?'

'Yes.' She held herself upright in her chair, hands clenched.

'I believe that you were one of Sylvie's closest friends?'

She nodded, not far from tears.

'Tell me what you told the sergeant about Saturday night.'

'About Sylvie leaving early?'

'Yes.'

'Well, there's a cloakroom at the Barn. I was just coming out of the loo and there was Sylvie putting her coat on. I said something like, "Had enough?" and she said, "You could say that". It didn't mean anything – just chat.'

'What time was this?'

'Before ten, say a quarter-to.'

'Did she seem worried or depressed?'

The girl hesitated. 'No, I don't think so. She wasn't exactly swinging but Sylvie was always a bit moody. I thought, perhaps, she had to go home early because of her dad.'

'When you went back to the Barn was Peters there?'

'I don't know.' The translucent skin of her forehead wrinkled into a frown. 'I don't think he was.'

'Did you see him again that evening?'

She shook her head. 'It's no good, I don't think so but I'm not sure.'

'Never mind. What about Clarissa?'

'No, Clarissa wasn't there definitely. She didn't come in at all on Saturday evening.'

'Was that unusual?'

'No, she often doesn't come in and when she does she doesn't stay long. I don't think she cares for it all that much.'

'Have you any idea where Sylvie was going when she left?'

'No, I told you, I thought she was going home.'

'Could she have arranged to meet someone?'

'But who?'

'Wasn't she friendly with Jackie Martin, the schoolteacher?'

Sally shook her head with decision. 'She wouldn't have been going to meet Jackie, that was ancient history.'

Wycliffe was smoking his pipe, the atmosphere was becoming more relaxed, the girl had got over her nervousness and was starting to talk naturally. 'Of course, she couldn't quite shake him off, he kept hanging around. Sometimes he would wait for her when she was at the Barn.'

'And she objected?'

'Well, he was a bit of a pest. All the same I felt sorry for him. Sylvie didn't mince words.'

'But he persisted?'

'Yes.'

'He must have been very fond of her.'

She nodded gravely. 'Yes, I think Sylvie was the only girl who ever took any notice of him and when she ditched him . . .'

'Jackie isn't very popular with girls?'

She grinned briefly. 'He hasn't got a clue! I don't know what it is about him really but he's so *serious* . . . He puts you off.'

'Would it be right to say that Sylvie broke it off with Jackie because she became attached to Peters?'

She considered this. 'I suppose it would. She fell for Vince in a big way, there's no doubt about that.'

'And she wasn't the only one, apparently.'

'That's true. Apart from all the glamour – him being who he is and all that – he's still quite a nice bloke to be with. He can make you *feel* somebody when he puts his mind to it . . .'

'Is it true that he has sex with several of the girls?'

Again the frown. 'I know that's what they say but I think all that talk is exaggerated.'

'By whom?'

She looked surprised. 'Why, by the girls. It's the thing to say.'

'A sort of status symbol?'

'Something like that.'

'What about Sylvie?'

She thought for some time before answering. 'In Sylvie's case I think there was something in it. Vince treated her a bit different from the others. Of course, I don't *know* anything. Sylvie wasn't the sort to talk.'

And that was all. Trinity House were able to confirm that the fog did not really thicken until after midnight. The signals on Temple Rock and Ship Island were logged at 01.07 and 01.11 respectively. In his mind's eye Wycliffe could see the young people setting off home in the moist darkness, shouting to each other, laughing. Where was Sylvie then?

Wycliffe and Gill interviewed Jackie Martin together. He was a tall, thin, studious-looking youth with glasses and he walked with a stoop as though to minimize his height. He looked pale and ill and his movements were jerky – unpredictable.

'Not the first time you've been in this room, Mr Martin?'

'What?' He looked round vaguely.

'You teach in the school, don't you?'

'Oh, yes, I see what you mean.'

'What do you teach?'

'Biology.'

'Sylvie's death must have come as a great shock to you.'

He nodded, dumbly.

'Did you know she was pregnant?'

He shook his head decisively. 'No, I didn't know – not until her father told me yesterday.'

'Is it possible that you were the child's father?'

He flushed. 'Me? No! We . . . Sylvie and I never . . .'

'Have you any idea whose child it might be?'

'No, none.'

'Are you saying that Sylvie would go with anybody?'

'No! I'm not saying that.' He picked at a loose thread in the seam of his trousers. 'I suppose it must have been Peters' child.'

'You are a friend of his?'

'Not a friend.'

'But you visit him.'

'We have a common interest but I don't like him very much. At least I don't like some of the things he does . . .'

'Such as?'

He shifted uneasily in his chair, apparently in an agony of discomfort. 'He had sexual relations with several of the girls.'

'With Sylvie too?'

'Yes.'

'Was that why you and Sylvie broke it off?'

He blushed again. 'When she met Peters she didn't want me any more.' His humility was embarrassing.

'What is your common interest with Peters?'

'We are both interested in the Diptera – the two-winged flies.'

Gill, who had not so far spoken, stretched his legs and asked lazily, 'Don't all flies have two wings?'

'True flies do but there are many insects loosely called flies which have four wings.'

'Well I'm damned!' Gill said without a smile.

'What do you do with these flies?'

'We collect and study them – there are five thousand species in Great Britain and eighty thousand in the whole world . . .'

'And Peters is interested in these insects?'

'Oh, yes. He studied zoology at University and he was going to specialize in entomology but he got mixed up in this pop music . . .'

'Did you go to University, Mr Martin?'

'No, I wasn't good enough. I trained to teach at a College of Education.'

Gill leaned forward as though much interested. 'Although Peters took your girl away from you, you still visit him?'

Martin looked surprised. 'I told you, we are both interested in flies.'

'Where were you on Saturday evening?'

'Why do you ask me that?'

Wycliffe was reassuring. 'We ask every witness that question and later today we shall start to ask everyone in the island.'

'Oh, I see. I was at home.'

'All the evening?'

'Yes.'

'Anyone to confirm that?'

'My mother, I suppose.'

'You and your mother live alone?' Wycliffe was convinced that the boy's mother would turn out to be a widow. He was wrong.

'My father is there too but he's an invalid, almost helpless.'

Wycliffe thought he could sense the claustrophobic atmosphere of the home which had produced this sensitive, slightly effeminate and pedantic young man.

'Even after your relationship with Sylvie ended you sometimes waited for her when she was at the Barn?'

It was painful to watch him. His hands gripped his knees, the knuckles showing white. 'That's my business!'

'Yes. But did you meet her on Saturday night?'

'No, I did not!' He almost shouted. 'I told you, I was home all the evening.' He stood up, looking round the room wildly as though he could not remember where the exit was. 'Oh, God! Why do you have to keep on and on?' He burst into tears and rushed out of the room.

'Let him go!'

'Bloody little drip!' Gill said.

Wycliffe sighed. 'We can't all have heads and hides like rugby footballs, Jimmy.'

Wycliffe was interested in going through the reports to come across Marsden's statement. Nicholas Jason Marsden, aged sixty-one of Quay Cottages, Quincey Cove. Occupation: Fisherman. The statement merely confirmed what he had told Wycliffe the previous night. Wycliffe asked Jordan about him.

'The Marsden family is our cross, sir. They've lived out to Quincey Cove for a hundred and fifty years and now there's five generations of them, living. Old Emily must be knocking on for the century and there's Moira who's fifteen so it won't be long before we've got six generations to contend with. Nick is the oldest living male – the women always outlive the men by twenty years at least.'

'What do they all do for a living – fish?'

Jordan scratched his ear. 'A good question. Of course, they've got their pots . . .'

'Pots?'

'Crab and lobster, sir. They do a bit of long lining too but that's not the half of it. Where there's pickings, there you'll find a Marsden and what they can't get any other way, they'll nick.'

'Has he got form?'

'Not half what he should have – bound over in sixty-three, three months in sixty-five and a year in seventy.'

'He seems to hang around the youngsters who go to the Barn.'

'I agree he's a bit of a Peeping Tom but I think he's harmless from that point of view.'

'I hope you're right! So you wouldn't look on him as a good witness?'

Jordan laughed. 'I wouldn't believe him if he told me the time. Lying comes more natural than the truth from the Marsdens. They're all alike.'

'Has he any special reason to have it in for Peters?'

'I'll say! Peters owns all the land down the valley to the cove and he's trying to get the Marsdens out.'

'Seems a bit hard after a hundred and fifty years.'

Jordan hesitated, torn between local loyalties and sweet reason. 'It is hard but Peters has a point. He never gets any rent – not that he seems to care about that, but he's keen to have the cove tidied up. It's a pretty spot and Marsden's place is surrounded by all the junk in creation, piles of drift-wood, scrap, staved-in boats, oil drums, beds, mattresses – you name it, he's got it. Peters gave him six months to get it tidied up and when nothing happened he applied for a possession order. It comes up in a fortnight's time.'

'Marsden seems to get on well enough with Peters' brother.'

'Oh, he does that all right and it's not so surprising as it sounds. If you ask me the Peters brothers don't hit it off. Roger stays at a café on the quay when he's in the islands and I don't think he sees much of his brother.'

Deputy Chief Constable Bellings telephoned.

'So it's murder, Charles.'

'It looks like it.' Wycliffe was always at his most boorish with the suave, politically-minded Bellings.

'What does the Lord Warden have to say about that?'

'I've no idea, I haven't asked him.'

'You mean you haven't made contact? You should, Charles, you really should. Sir John's influence isn't confined to the islands, he's a man to be reckoned with. What about this fellow Peters?'

'What about him?'

'He's evidently a thorn in the flesh of the locals.'

'But that doesn't make him a murderer.'

'No, of course not. Anyway, don't neglect Sir John, the Chief would be most upset if he thought . . .'

Being a detective has its dramatic moments but mostly it is boring routine; asking dull questions and getting dull answers, making and reading endless reports, talking to people who are frightened and suspicious or cunning and deceitful. And after all that you have to keep your superiors happy, the worst chore of all.

The midday boat brought a police Land-Rover and a number of reinforcements, a mixed bag, drawn from several divisions, in the charge of an inspector. After a meal they were put to work on house-to-house enquiries. 'Where were you on Saturday evening between seven-thirty and midnight? Did you know Sylvia Eva? When did you last see her? Have you seen her recently in company with a man? Have you seen . . . ? Do you know . . . ? Will you let us know if . . . ?' The answers were laboriously written down and some of them were afterwards typed with carbon copies to swell the files.

Wycliffe had a canteen meal with Chief Inspector Gill and the newly arrived Inspector Golly. Golly had a protruding Adam's apple and a jet black military moustache; he wore bandbox uniform and held himself like a guardsman. Wycliffe felt an irrational dislike. The meal was depressing – fish cooked in batter with tinned peas and pulpy tomatoes.

'I am at your disposal, sir.'

Wycliffe looked at him blandly and said nothing.

'If you will give me your instructions, sir.'

'I am going to put you in charge of paper, Mr Golly. It will be up to you to collect it, read what is on it and decide what to do with it.'

'You want me to be a collator for the case, sir.'

'You have an apt turn of phrase, Mr Golly,' Wycliffe said gravely.

In the afternoon Inspector Golly came to see Wycliffe; he stood in the office, waiting to be addressed. Although it was stickily hot he was still wearing full uniform.

'Mr Golly?'

'I thought you should see this, sir.' He placed two sheets of notepaper on the desk – a letter, beautifully written in italic script. 'It's young Martin's writing, sir, I checked.'

The letter was undated and bore no address. It read:

My dearest Sylvie,

I am forced to write to you because you will never let me see you alone. I have tried to accept that all is over between us and to resign myself to seeing you give yourself to someone else; someone who, in the long run, is sure to hurt you. I think I could bear losing you if it meant your happiness but you know in your heart that it does not, that you are to him only what others have been and will be.

I do not ask you to love me, only that you will let me see you sometimes. I will do anything you say, accept any conditions you make if you will only give me a little hope. If you will not, I do not think that I shall be able to carry on living. During the precious time that we were together you became so much a part of me that I cannot now truly exist without you. I lie awake at night, I cannot eat and I cannot work, for you are always in my mind and your dear face is always before my eyes. If you have any kindness left for me let me talk to you, my darling. I will wait for you tomorrow night as so many times before but this time in the hope that you will take pity on me.

Counting the hours and the minutes, my love.

J.

As Wycliffe finished reading Gill came in, just back from the inquest.

'How did it go?'

'Very businesslike. Evidence of the finding of the body, identification and adjournment. No messing. The funeral is tomorrow.'

Wycliffe passed him the letter. Gill read it and dropped it on the desk with an amused leer on his face. He had never needed to beg of any woman; his ugly, expressive features and his blatant sexuality seemed to be irresistible. 'Martin?'

Wycliffe nodded.

'Well, I've told you what I think of him. Where did it come from anyway?'

'Sergeant Scales found it in the girl's bedroom, in a pocket of one of her coats. I brought it along to Mr Wycliffe at once.'

As a matter of routine, Wycliffe had given instructions for Sylvie's bedroom to be searched.

'No date,' Gill said.

'But there's an envelope with a postmark.' Inspector Golly produced the envelope like a conjurer.

Gill took it. 'Is this a bloody lucky dip? What are we supposed to do next? Guess what you've got in the other pocket?'

Golly stiffened but said nothing. Wycliffe was having trouble keeping his pipe alight. Gill put the envelope on the desk.

'It's postmarked six o'clock Friday evening so she got it on Saturday morning. That boy conned us, she left early to meet him.'

'Or not to,' Wycliffe said.

'I don't get it.'

'I'm saying that it's equally possible she left early to avoid him.'

Gill slumped on to one of the chairs by Wycliffe's desk. 'You may be right at that! Either way the lad's got some talking to do. We'd better have him in.'

'See him at home first.' In Wycliffe's experience there was much to be gained from seeing a man in his normal surroundings. There might come a time when it would be good psychology to bring him into the neutral or even hostile context of an interview room but it was a mistake to start there. It was for this reason – at least, with this excuse, that he insisted on going out and seeing for himself. 'Where does he live?'

'The Tower House on the quay, sir.' Golly had only been in the islands a few hours but he had taken the trouble to brief himself from the case records.

'Thank you, Mr Golly.'

Gill's face was one broad, sardonic grin.

Wycliffe went down the steep slope from the school to the quay. At the peak of the season the *Islander* brought day trippers from the mainland; eight hours on the water, four on the island. She was lying at her berth and her returning passengers were straggling up the gangway. Charlie Martin was sitting on his bollard, smoking his pipe. He looked at Wycliffe, his serene blue eyes, speculative, appraising.

'No arrest yet, Mr Wycliffe?'

'Not yet, Mr Martin.'

The old man studied the bowl of his pipe thoughtfully then raised his eyes to Wycliffe's. 'I suppose it's possible that the lass had an accident after all?' He asked the question with disarming naïvety.

Wycliffe was puzzled. 'If so it was a very odd sort of accident.'

Martin nodded. 'It's odd how people fall. I remember a case when I was a young man – fifty years ago . . .' And he launched into a tedious anecdote about a mate of his who had fallen from the crosstrees to the deck of a wind-jammer. Such loquacity was uncharacteristic and obviously had a motive though Wycliffe was not sure what the motive was. He excused himself at last and continued along the quay.

The Tower House was the folly of a well-to-do oddity who had settled on the island in the 1830s when the islanders scraped a living out of a traditional blend of primitive cultivation, equally primitive fishing and better organized smuggling. The house stood apart from others along the quay; it was four storeys high, octagonal in shape and surmounted by a cupola of sheet lead turned almost white by the weather and bird droppings. The tower was neglected, with stucco peeling off the walls and the woodwork destitute of any sign of paint.

Wycliffe knocked on the door which opened on to the street. After a short while his knock was answered by a woman in her late forties. She was thin, wiry and tough with the look of one who has survived more than her fair share of adversity. She was wiping rough, reddened hands on a white towel.

'Yes?'
'Mrs Martin?'
'What do you want?'
Wycliffe introduced himself although he was sure that she knew him and said that he had come to talk to her son.
'About the Eva girl?'
'About Sylvie, yes.'
She sniffed. 'I don't know why you have to keep pestering my son, he's upset enough already.'
'Is he at home?'
She hesitated then bowed to the inevitable. 'Yes, he is. You had better come in.'
If the outside of the house was neglected the inside was spartan but scrupulously clean. The little hall was floored with red quarry tiles, worn but shining and the wooden, spiral staircase was covered with polished linoleum held in place by gleaming, brass stair-rods. A single door off the hall stood partly open into the living-room and Wycliffe glimpsed an old-fashioned range and, seated beside it in a slatted wooden armchair, an incredibly thin old man with paper-white features and lifeless, staring eyes which seemed disproportionately large. She pulled the door to quickly, shutting out the image.
'My son's room is on the top floor, I'll take you up.'
Wycliffe protested that he could find his own way and after a moment of doubt she agreed. 'A remarkable house you have, Mrs Martin.'
'It's cheap.'
It was not until he had turned the spiral, out

of sight of the hall, that he heard her open the living-room door and her dry, aggressive voice saying, 'It's nothing, don't excite yourself. Just somebody to see Jackie.'

One room on each floor. The doors set deeply in the thick walls, each in a Gothic arch like the doors in a church. Although Martin must have heard him climbing the stairs he gave no sign until Wycliffe knocked at the door of his room.

'Come in.'

The landing and stairs had been cut off in such a way that the room had seven sides, three of them had windows and the others were lined with bookshelves and cupboards. As Wycliffe entered, Martin got up from a table near the middle of the room where he must have been sitting, brooding for there was nothing on the table. He looked even more pale and pinched than he had done in the morning and his eyes behind the glasses were red rimmed.

'I'm sorry about this morning, I couldn't help it.'

Wycliffe was drawn, irresistibly, to the windows and stood, with his back to the room, staring out over the harbour, the shallow bay and the open sea beyond. 'What a view!'

'What? Oh, yes, I suppose it is pretty impressive if you're not used to it.'

Wycliffe continued to stand by the window and the silence lengthened. Martin fidgeted until he could stand it no longer and burst out, 'What do you want? Why have you come here?'

Wycliffe did not answer immediately but after a little while he said, quietly, 'You know that Sylvie was murdered?'

Martin laughed, almost hysterically. 'You believe that?'

'I know it to be a fact.' He turned to face the young man.

'They said that to make trouble for Peters.' He was standing, gripping the edge of the table with both hands. 'They want to get him off the island.'

'It's not a question of what anybody said. Somebody killed Sylvie by beating her across the head and face with a weapon of some sort; then, and not until then, her body was pushed into the quarry.'

He thought Martin was going to faint and guided him to a chair. The boy collapsed into it and sat with his eyes closed. Wycliffe drew up the only other chair and sat near him.

'You were very much in love with Sylvie weren't you?'

The eyelids flickered but there was no other response. Wycliffe knew enough of human nature to recognize that his collapse was half genuine, half a protective sham. The boy was near the end of his tether but he was prepared to make himself appear worse than he was in order to avoid questions.

As Wycliffe took the letter from his pocket Martin's eyes opened.

'From you to Sylvie, written the day before she was murdered and arranging to meet her on Saturday evening when she left the Barn . . .'

'You have no right!' His anger flared and died.

Wycliffe leaned forward in his chair and spoke with great gravity. 'Sooner or later you will have to tell me what happened on Saturday night.'

'Nothing happened. I told you, I was here all the evening.'

'You did not keep the appointment you made?'

'No!' Defiant.

'That is a lie!'

Martin sat motionless and was silent. The windows were open and the noises of the waterfront drifted up to them. The *Islander* gave a short blast on her siren to warn latecomers, gulls shrieked, the engine of a motor launch spluttered into life. It was even possible to hear the words of two tourists discussing whether or not they would go on an evening cruise round the island.

'What do you want me to say?'

'I want you to tell me the truth about Saturday night.'

'You won't believe me.'

Wycliffe said nothing.

'Sylvie usually left the Barn at about eleven o'clock, sometimes later.'

'Well?'

'I left home about ten and I got there by half-past.'

'Where?'

'Where I had waited for her before, at the top of the slope above the valley.'

'Near the quarry?'

'Fairly near, I suppose.'

'What happened?'

He shook his head. 'Nothing happened. I waited there until they broke up and they all came up the hill together. Sylvie wasn't with them.'

'How could you know? It was dark.'

'I would have recognized her.'

'Did any of them see you?'

'I don't think so.'

'What did you do?'

Another long silence.

'Well?'

'I went down to the house. The Barn was in darkness but there was a light in the living-room at the back of the house. The curtains were drawn and I couldn't see anything.'

'Then?'

'Nothing. I thought she must be with Peters so I came home.'

It was so fatuous that it had the ring of truth. 'Is that the truth?'

'I swear it!'

'What time did you get home?'

'A quarter-to-one or a little after.'

'How long did it take you?'

'A bit longer than usual because of the fog – about three-quarters of an hour.'

Fact or fiction? By leaning on the boy a bit harder he might find out but it was too early. When he put pressure on a suspect he liked to have most of the cards already in his hand.

He pottered about the room trying to get the measure of its owner. A fairly catholic collection of books. Natural history, entomology, evolution and genetics. A few books on archaeology and history, some popular works on psychology and shelf after shelf of historical romances from Dumas to du Maurier. Martin's insect collection was housed in a stack of cork-lined boxes and he had an old-fashioned binocular microscope with a brass tube.

Wycliffe had sensed the claustrophobic atmosphere in which Martin lived, now he was struck by the introverted character of the room. It was a severely circumscribed world, a cell, a cocoon, almost complete in itself – almost but not quite. Martin had to venture out, not only to earn his living but to give substance to his romantic dream. That had been Sylvie's role and she had let him down.

'While you were waiting for Sylvie did you see anyone?'

'No, well, only Nick Marsden. He was mooning about as usual. I didn't take much notice.'

'I would like you to come back with me to make a statement.'

He looked at Wycliffe with frightened eyes. 'Shall I be free to go afterwards?'

'Why not?'

As Wycliffe went out on to the landing he saw Mrs Martin disappearing round the bend of the stairs but when they reached the ground floor the living-room door was closed. Martin hesitated. 'I'd better tell her . . .'

He went into the living-room, closing the door behind him but he was only gone for a short time. They walked along the quay and up the slope to the school. Martin walked self-consciously in company with the chief superintendent as though all eyes were on him. Charlie Martin saw them pass but he gave no sign.

'Has your father been an invalid for long?'

'Eleven years. Of course, he's a lot older than mother, he'll be seventy-two next month if he lives that long. I don't know how she . . .'

'You were saying?'

'Nothing.'

They reached the school entrance and as they passed through the swing-doors Wycliffe said, 'By the way, Mr Martin, do you happen to know your blood group?'

Martin seemed surprised by the question. 'Group O – why?'

Wycliffe was saved explanation by several pressmen waiting for him in the foyer.

Jackie Martin spent the evening in his room. He tried to work on his insects, then he tried to read but he found himself going over and over the same lines. He looked out of the window and saw in the eastern sky a pale reflection of the sunset. As usual on a fine summer evening the quay was crowded with people and their voices reached him – normal, cheerful voices, the voices of people quietly enjoying themselves. Boys arm in arm with scantily clad girls. He watched, half yearning, half contemptuous. Sometimes he felt that he would give ten years of his life to change places with any one of them.

Not for the first time he thought about suicide. His memory was well stocked with literary and historical suicides but when it came to the point he found himself ignorant. How to set about it? He could not face pain, nor could he contemplate those awful moments which must come to a drowning man when he begins to suffocate . . . The immediate response must be to breathe . . . In his imagination he lived through such moments and groaned aloud. He told himself that he was not afraid of death, death seemed almost friendly but dying . . .

He had to talk to somebody or he would go mad. Not his mother. He could not face another confrontation which would end, inevitably, with them wallowing in each other's emotions. Afterwards he would feel drained – physically and mentally.

He put on his jacket and crept downstairs but as he reached the little hall the door of the living-room opened.

'Where are you going?'

'Out.'

She looked at him for a moment in silence as though trying to make up her mind then she kissed him on the cheek and let him go. 'Be careful!'

For once it was better outside.

He walked up the hill and out of the town on to the moor. It was dusk and growing dark. He hurried as though he had a pressing appointment and only slowed when he came in sight of Salubrious Place. There was nobody in the Barn and the house showed only a single light. His courage all but failed him, he almost turned back.

When he rang it was not long before a light went on in the hall and Clarissa answered the door.

'Jackie!' She sounded surprised but not unwelcoming. 'Come into the living-room.'

Vince was sitting at a table on which playing cards were laid out. The big room was lit only by a standard lamp near the table and the curtains had not been drawn over the great wall of glass which separated the room from the meadow. The last vestiges of daylight were fading from a cloudless sky.

'We are playing Bezique and I am winning so Vince will be glad to stop.'

Vince's greeting was cool.

'Don't let me stop the game.'

'Don't be silly! We will play three-handed bridge,' Clarissa said.

And they did. For a time Jackie came near to feeling normal. Until he noticed the way Vince was looking at him. There was no mistaking that look, he had been on the receiving end too often. Later, Clarissa switched on the lights, drew the curtains and brought in tea and little pâté sandwiches. Then he had to go. Vince saw him to the door. In the hall Vince gave him a deliberate, detached, speculative look. 'You haven't got the guts to go through with it, have you?'

It was after midnight when he let himself into the Tower House. The door creaked but he shut it quickly behind him almost as though he were afraid that he had been followed. After the soft, balmy night air the cold, close and humid darkness in the little stone hallway might have repelled him but now it seemed like a welcome. He crept up the stairs. The door on the first landing where his father and mother slept was a little open and the pale yellow beam of the nightlight reached out across the red tiles. He could hear the shallow, wheezy, tremulous breathing of his sleeping father. How often had he listened to it wishing that it would stop for ever? His father's senile petulance, his slobbering habits, his incontinence, frightened and sickened him. They were a persistent, intrusive nastiness too close to the core of his life. But now he had other things on his mind.

He continued up the steps to his own room. He did not switch on the light but sat in a chair by one of the windows. The night was full of stars and the room was full of shadows with pale highlights like reflections in a mirror. All his life he had been a victim. As a schoolboy he had been the butt of other boys, the one who always tried not to be noticed and rarely succeeded. To please his mother he had become, of all things, a schoolteacher and narrowly avoided being the victim of his pupils by ingratiating himself with them at the expense of work and true discipline. Slowly and painfully he had acquired, layer by layer, a protective skin; now it had been stripped away and he was vulnerable as never before.

He could still see the look on Peters' face.

His eyes filled with the burning tears of self-pity and he began to sob helplessly. His mother came in. She stood over his chair and cushioned his head against her breast, stroking his hair and murmuring consolation. 'Oh my boy! Oh my boy!'

Chapter Five

Wednesday was another fine day. Wycliffe woke early to the now familiar pattern of dancing wavelets reflected on the ceiling. Charlie Martin was in his usual place with his little black book and the tanker waggon was refuelling the boats. A few visitors were about, taking a walk before breakfast, trying to glimpse something of the real life of the island as one goes back-stage at a theatre.

When he went downstairs the Jordans were already at breakfast – grilled mackerel, caught that morning.

'You were talking about Peters' brother last night, sir.'

'I saw him in the bar with Nick Marsden – what about him?'

Jordan wiped his lips with an outsized table napkin. 'He's an odd sort of chap, spends a lot of time on the island. God knows what he does for a living.'

Wycliffe waited while Mrs Jordan slipped another freshly grilled fish on her husband's plate. 'The point is, as I told you, he doesn't live at Salubrious Place, he lodges with Wendy Hicks, the widow woman who runs the Quay Café.'

Mrs Jordan made a curious, disapproving noise

and Jordan laughed. 'You can see what the women think of her but she seems to be the attraction. But apart from all that the brother seems a decent enough chap and he gets on well with most of the locals – the men, anyway.'

Wycliffe was having difficulty in removing the bones from his fish and he made no reply.

By the time he set out for his headquarters the quay was busy. He went into the shop for some tobacco and queued with the tourists who wanted their morning papers. He was conscious of being pointed out by the knowledgeable to the uninformed. News of the murder had reached the tourists mainly through the London dailies for the islanders were disinclined to discuss their domestic affairs with foreigners. The little man behind the counter reached past two customers in front of Wycliffe to hand him his tobacco. 'The usual, Chief Superintendent!' Wycliffe growled unpleasantly.

The improvised headquarters was running smoothly thanks to Gill. Wycliffe had no organizing flair but to Gill organization came as naturally as breathing. The atmosphere was businesslike, everyone busy, nobody flustered; tables and desks were uncluttered and files in constant use were housed on trolleys which had been borrowed from the canteen. All of which was surprising when one looked at Gill himself; ungainly, slovenly in dress, he never stood if he could sit or sat if he could sprawl.

Wycliffe spent half an hour going through the reports. Nothing much. The constable who had been on watch at Salubrious Place reported seeing Jackie Martin leaving the house at 11.30 the previous night.

The constable's turn of duty had started at 10.00 so that Jackie must have arrived before then.

After going through the reports he held a conference in his office; Chief Inspector Gill and Inspector Golly. The three principals had identical files. Wycliffe lit his pipe, Gill was smoking a cheroot. Golly sat upright in his chair and waited to be addressed.

'You first, Jimmy.'

'I don't suppose you want statistics of the house to house reports and the circulars?'

'Not really.'

Gill grinned and turned over several pages of his file. 'Mr Golly has had them all nicely typed out.' He flicked the long ash from his cheroot vaguely in the direction of the ashtray on Wycliffe's desk. 'Half the males in the island, tourists and locals alike, seem unable to give a precise and/or substantiated account of their whereabouts and activities on Saturday night.'

'Get on with it, Jimmy!'

Gill stretched out his long legs. 'It comes to this: it's possible that we have some sort of kink loose on the island who gets his kicks from knocking off girls after dark. If it's one of those we shall soon know, but I don't think so and neither do you.'

'No, I agree, it hasn't got the marks. Mr Golly?'

Golly seemed startled by the implied question. 'I don't know, sir. I wouldn't like to give an opinion at this stage.'

Gill opened his mouth to say something scathing but, catching Wycliffe's eye, changed his mind. 'The crime we've got on our hands probably runs true to type. The kid got herself slugged because she was involved in an emotional mess. She was probably the cause of it, she probably enjoyed being in it, but she didn't think anybody was going to take it seriously enough to slug her if she stirred it up a bit more. Silly little bitch! They ask for it!' Gill, though apparently happily married, never missed a chance to preach his gospel against womankind, or, at least, against emotional involvement with women. He turned to Golly with a ferocious grin. 'Sometimes I think you're better off with a nice, clean-living young man.'

The inspector smiled doubtfully.

Gill went on, 'Where does that get us? As far as we know the two chaps she was involved with were Peters and Martin. Neither of them can give a satisfactory account of himself for the relevant times on Saturday night. Let's start with Peters. In his statement he says that he left the Barn at a little before ten. He had a headache and he went for a walk. Down the valley to the sea, up on to the cliffs and back over the moor by the usual path to the house. When he got back the kids had gone. Apparently it was nothing unusual for them to be left to pack up. One of them would lock the Barn door and hang the key on a hook just inside the front door of the house. Ma'moiselle Loiseau says that her lord and master came in at five minutes after midnight.' Gill looked from Wycliffe to Golly and back again. 'Walking for two bloody hours over rough country in the dark! It's so bloody stupid it might even be true but, of course, there's not a scrap of corroboration.' He rifled through a few more pages of the file.

'And here is Master Martin's contribution. He left home to meet his girl friend at five minutes to ten. He reached the appointed spot at about half-past and hung about there until the party in the Barn broke up and the kids went home. Mark you, he didn't trouble himself to ask one of them what had happened to Sylvie. He assumed that she was with Peters and he went down to the house. According to him he loitered around the back of the house for some time, then he got tired and went home, reaching there at a quarter to one.' Gill slapped the file shut. 'Marvellous, isn't it? And not a shred of evidence to support that load of crap either.'

Wycliffe had listened without comment and without much apparent interest. Now he turned to Inspector Golly, 'Anything to say about that, Mr Golly?'

The inspector braced himself. 'Two things strike me, sir. First, if the dead girl was having an affair with Peters she could have aroused the jealousy of Peters' mistress . . .'

'You think so?' Gill was ironic.

Golly ignored him. 'According to Peters' story, the Loiseau girl must have been alone for the whole evening. Peters was at the Barn until ten and after that he was walking on the moor until midnight.'

'The point being?'

'That Miss Loiseau had, not only a credible motive, but also an opportunity to commit the crime.' Golly felt the need to define his position more clearly. 'I am not saying that the young lady is a murderess, only that even when we limit the choice of culprit to those emotionally involved with the dead girl she cannot be excluded.'

'I think you put that rather well, Mr Golly.'

'Now for my second point. I believe that Dr Ross put the time of death at between eleven and twelve – not earlier.'

'Well?'

'Martin admits to having been in the vicinity of the quarry from half-past ten until the young people left the Barn at half-past eleven. Peters, whether or not he took the walk he describes, could have been there at the relevant time and, if he is telling the truth, he *must* have been there at some time shortly before midnight.'

'You are saying that both of them could . . .' But Golly would not allow himself to be interrupted.

'I am saying more than that, Mr Gill, if you will allow me to finish. After half-past eleven Martin says that he walked down to the house, loitered round the back for a while then walked home, arriving there around a quarter to one having taken three-quarters of an hour on the way. Surely it is remarkable that Martin and Peters do not appear to have met?'

'You've got a point!' Gill admitted generously. 'A good point.'

'In other words,' Wycliffe said, 'it seems that they can't both be telling the truth and that's always something.'

'In my opinion all we need do is to lean on 'em a bit. The two of them together don't add up to one good man.'

Wycliffe knocked out his pipe into the ashtray.

'They won't run away, Jimmy, and before we commit ourselves I'd like to feel a good deal surer of my ground.'

'You're worried about motive?'

'Partly, yes.'

The chief inspector lit another cheroot and puffed lazily. 'My money is on Martin and he seems to have had motive enough. I don't think he planned to kill the girl but when he met her it's more than likely that her attitude brought his jealousy and frustration to flash point. As far as Peters is concerned . . .'

The telephone rang and Wycliffe answered it. The Lord Warden would be grateful if Mr Wycliffe could find time to lunch with him. A launch would be at the Seymour Steps at 12.00 noon.

A Royal Command. Wycliffe grumbled. He had no social aspirations and he had never been a golf-and-country-club copper. That was why he would remain stuck at his present rank and why he thought himself lucky to have got so far. He had no grievance. He was a Jack and he wanted to stay that way. Nowadays it was difficult above the rank of detective inspector but by being bloody minded, good at his job, and by carefully cultivating a reputation for eccentricity, he had managed it – more or less. If you wanted 'in' at the administrative level you had to mix with the administrators. That was reasonable. He didn't.

'What's he called?'

Inspector Golly looked mildly surprised and reproving. 'Sir John Gordon – quite a notability. He had a distinguished career in the Diplomatic Service before he succeeded his father here. Everybody was surprised when he gave it up on his father's death. The post of Lord Warden is hereditary but there is no obligation to reside here . . .'

'Really! Thank you Mr Golly.' Another aspiring chief constable.

Wycliffe stood up. 'Getting back to the case, we need more facts. Follow up the time angle. Somebody must have seen young Martin leave to keep his appointment, just possibly somebody saw him coming back. God knows what goes on after dark in this place. It seems that Nick Marsden was out on the moor – was anybody else? Somebody might have seen Peters. The place seems to be plagued by naturalists – don't any of them keep the silent watches of the night?'

Gill knew if Golly did not that there would be no more discussion. It was rare for Wycliffe to take part in more than a brief exchange of views. He had said more than once that other people's ideas only confused him.

Inspector Golly ventured, 'The house-to-house and the questionnaire both appear to have covered the ground pretty well, sir . . .'

'No doubt, Mr Golly, no doubt, but look into it. Mr Gill will put you on the right lines. Thank you.'

Golly, who thought that he had made a good first impression, now began to wonder.

Perhaps it was because Jimmy Gill's view of the case came so close to his own that he had refused to hear any more. He had, as often before, the feeling that it was too soon to jump to any conclusion but he would have found it difficult to offer any logical objection to action if he had allowed the discussion to develop. He was restless and the very atmosphere of routine efficiency in his headquarters oppressed him. It is easy to be superbly efficient in gathering, classifying and filing damn-all. Most offices specialize in it.

He washed behind his ears, combed his hair and stole guiltily out of the building and escaped down on to the quay. There were not many people about. The pleasure boats had already left for the off-islands and the *Islander* had not yet arrived with its day-trippers. Half-a-dozen men with a council lorry were erecting scaffold poles in barrels of sand at intervals along the quay. Carnival Week was due to start that evening with a grand procession.

Uncertain of the licensing hours or whether the islands were troubled by such things, he walked in the direction of the Seymour Arms and found the bars open. In the public one of the boatmen was drinking with Nick Marsden. The landlord was reading a newspaper spread out on the bar. Marsden acknowledged Wycliffe with a diffident glance and a few moments later he and his companion drank up and left.

The landlord was patronizing. 'Making progress, sir?'

'Of a sort.'

'It's difficult for an outsider. Impossible, I'd say.'

Wycliffe ordered a pint. 'Have one with me.' He lit his pipe. 'That was Nick Marsden wasn't it? He seems quite a character.'

'He's clever.'

'Clever?'

The landlord drew a pint and placed it on the counter. 'How do you make your living, Mr Wycliffe?'

'Work for it, I suppose.'

The landlord nodded. 'So do I. Nick Marsden hasn't done a week's work in forty years but he doesn't go short of his beer or his baccy and his belly is never empty.'

'I see what you mean. It must be a knack.'

'If it is, all the Marsdens must have it, they're born scroungers.' The landlord drew a second pint. 'There's a whole clan of 'em over to Quincey Cove. Nick and me went to school together and I know the breed. Cheers!' He blew the froth off his beer and drank half of it.

'Apart from his scrounging, what sort of chap is he?'

The landlord gave him a sly look. 'I know what you're thinking but all I can say is I've never known Nick to be violent, he isn't that sort. As a boy you might say he was a bit of a coward. He used to get teased a lot because of the way he dressed but though he was big I never knew him to do anything about it . . . Of course, as a young man he was a great one for the women.' He took another gulp of beer and laughed. 'There's respectable grandmothers in this town today who couldn't lift their skirts fast enough for Nick when he was in his prime.'

'And now?'

The landlord made a gesture of contempt. 'Now he's just a dirty old man who gets his kicks watching the kids.'

'As long as he only watches.'

The landlord shrugged. 'She wasn't sexually assaulted, was she?'

There was silence for a time. When Wycliffe spoke again he changed the subject. 'It seems odd to me, the islanders have the reputation for not looking kindly on strangers and Vince Peters is a case in point. But Peters' brother isn't doing so badly from what I hear.'

The landlord gave him an appraising look. 'You've been getting around!' He finished his beer and wiped his lips. 'In this island, Mr Wycliffe, there's plenty of room at the bottom; you're only in trouble if you try to muscle in at the top.' He pushed his empty glass to one side and rested his arms on the bar. 'I wouldn't say this to anybody, Mr Wycliffe, but . . .' He got no further; his expression, which had been confiding, changed to one of professional geniality. 'Morning, Mr Martin.'

Charlie Martin had come in and was taking his usual seat. He looked depressed and his acknowledgement of Wycliffe's greeting was perfunctory.

When he had finished his drink Wycliffe went outside and stood with his arms resting on the rail staring into the harbour. He was trying to decide what colour the water was. Blue? Green? Blue-green? It was shot with gold – or yellow and the tip of each tiny ripple was silvered. If you added to that a certain indefinable translucency . . . He wondered too, why he had ever become a policeman and why a detective? He hadn't a clue what to do next.

He watched the *Islander* glide between the pier-heads and pass snugly into her berth. He watched the day-trippers stream off and immediately lay siege to the few shops on the quay. What came ye out into the wilderness to see?

A black launch with gleaming brasswork and white, coiled rope on the foc'sle slid into the harbour. There were two people in the well, the young man at the tiller in blue jersey and peaked cap and a dark girl in a flowered shirt and shorts. The helmsman cut back his motor, brought the launch round so that she glided to the steps and, as she did so, the girl stepped on to the gunnel and ashore in a single movement. She was up the steps on to the quay almost before the launch had come to rest.

'Superintendent Wycliffe?' The boatman held the launch to the steps with a boathook while he stepped aboard then, with a swirling wake, they were away across the harbour.

'I'm John Jenkins.'

Wycliffe had had nothing to do with the sea until he took up his west-country appointment four or five years previously and he had never ceased to be impressed by the skill and craft of those who lived by it.

'Who was the young lady?'

'Miss Gordon.'

The usual cagey, taciturn reception accorded to a stranger. This young man had an air of self-confidence, of true self-possession which he might have looked for in vain among the factory workers of his old manor. Perhaps he was romanticising but it seemed to him that our modern industrial society fails to provide the challenge which enables a man to find himself.

The town faces east, on one side of a narrow neck of land which juts out from the main body of the island. Morvyl lies away to the west and so they had to double Cligga Head at the northern tip of the promontory. As the launch came through the pier-heads John Jenkins opened the throttle and she charged into a surprisingly choppy sea, throwing up clouds of spray. The young man grinned, reached into the stern locker and handed him an oilskin coat. 'You'll get wet.'

They were running parallel with the coast and he could see the string of sandy coves, the low cliffs rising to the moor and the granite mass of Carngluze topping the lot and looking like an enchanted castle from a story book. As they approached the headland the cliffs became higher and steeper. Cligga itself rose sheer for ninety feet – not very high but impressive against the Lilliputian landscapes of the island. It was from Cligga that Sylvie's mother had fallen to her death and he could see the low platform of rock at the base which must be covered at high tide.

Off the headland there were cross currents which tumbled them a bit, then they were running into the sound which separates the island from Morvyl. The cliffs on either side were low and gentle with gorse and heather coming down almost to the tidemark. They made a broad sweep – to avoid a reef, John Jenkins said – then they crossed the sound and entered a tiny harbour with a few cottages backed by trees, a rare sight in the islands. They nosed their way through a clutter of small craft to the steps of a jetty. Wycliffe tried to step ashore with nonchalance if not with grace; for him the trip had not been long enough.

'You can't miss it, through the big gates and up the drive.'

The quay was almost deserted. Two old men on a seat seemed to be asleep and apart from them there was only a donkey in the shafts of a cart piled high with seaweed.

The gates at the end of the waterfront stood open between high granite pillars surmounted by carved beasts. He set off up the drive between masses of rhododendron and laurel. What impressed him was the silence. To the best of his recollection he had heard nothing but his own footfalls since John Jenkins had cut the engine. He saw little of the famous gardens for the drive ended suddenly in a gravelled area before the house. The house was nothing special, a gabled affair covered in creeper, which could have been built at any time in the fifty years before the first war. Wycliffe, who had a feeling for architecture, wondered what had been torn down to make way for it.

Everything went well enough. Sir John turned out, predictably, to be sixtyish, lean, bronzed, effortlessly courteous but not obtrusively Eton and New College. There was no sign of a Lady Gordon and they were only three to lunch, the third member of the party, a Dr Swann, an Oxford zoologist.

Wycliffe enjoyed his lunch, lentil soup flavoured with orange and coriander, a chicken salad and fruit. They drank a light, dry hock which had a faint bouquet of wild flowers. Gordon did the talking and he talked well, telling of his early years in the service which he had spent in Nanking when, despite Chiang Kai-shek's republic, the old China was still much in evidence. Wycliffe found himself thinking of Lamancha, Hannay and Sandy, the cult figures of the British hegemony. As a good socialist, Wycliffe disapproved but enjoyed himself all the same.

Afterwards they went out on to a terrace at the back of the house overlooking a small, formal garden. For the first time conversation turned to Sylvie's death.

'A tragic affair! . . . When I asked your chief for his help I had no idea it would turn out to be murder . . . This Peters fellow . . .'

Sir John spoke somewhat disjointedly with long pauses so that his hearers had plenty of time to match their own detail to his evocative outlines. It amounted to a rather skilful justification for the party line on Peters. 'We all want to preserve the beauty and character of the islands . . . They are so small . . .' With a sly twinkle in Swann's direction, 'It is a rather delicate exercise in conservation, you cannot risk the random importation of new, exotic species . . .'

A little more of the same and Sir John seemed to be hinting at what a happy solution it would be if it turned out that Peters had murdered Sylvie. 'Such an intractable young man! Not, perhaps, the best influence on our young people either . . . There have been times, I must confess, when I have had misgivings about my own daughter . . .'

Wycliffe pricked up his ears but nothing came of it. He began to wonder whether there was going to be any milk in the coconut. Perhaps it was only a social occasion. But it came.

'Actually, Dr Swann has something to tell you which you may think important . . .'

Swann was no conversationalist, he had contributed almost nothing to the talk so far. Wycliffe knew the type. A naturalist, happiest when human contacts could be cut to a minimum. He rather liked what he had seen of Swann but he was piqued at the way he had been lured into hearing evidence in a social context. Why couldn't the man have come to his headquarters like anybody else? There was a simple answer to that one – he was a friend of the Lord Warden. Wycliffe became terse and official.

'You are a naturalist?'

'Small mammals – rodent and shrews mainly. I'm doing a count among other things.'

'A count?'

'A census if you like. Population density in relation to habitat – that sort of thing. You won't want the details but it involves setting traps – live traps of course, and I make a point of inspecting my traps every six hours.'

'You work alone?'

'Always. I see enough of people during term time. My base is here, on Morvyl. I have a room with Ernie Stoffles and his wife. Ernie puts me ashore on the island of my choice with a little tent and enough food. I tell him to come back for me in three or four days – up to a week, depending on the size of the island and the variety of habitats which it offers.'

'And last week?'

'Last week I was camping near Salubrious Place,

a little way up the valley above the house. I was there from Monday to Sunday. Ernie took me off from Quincey Cove at about eight on Sunday morning. He was late because of the fog but by lunch-time I was on Menhegy.'

'You have something to tell me about Saturday night?' Wycliffe caught Gordon's eye. A very faint smile. He had got the message but it would make no difference. Paternalism is the kindest word for it and it may not be such a bad thing.

Swann was diffident. 'I doubt if it's important – only a snatch of conversation I happened to overhear – but I thought you had better be the judge. It was the girl's name – Sylvie – which made me wonder . . .' He uncrossed his legs and bent forward in his chair. 'I had set up my tent in a small clearing in the bracken about two hundred yards upstream from the bridge which leads to Salubrious Place. There's a path which runs by the stream up to the farm and, of course, it was a convenient spot for me, sheltered, plenty of water, and milk and eggs from the farm. After dark I usually settle down to get what sleep I can between visits to my traps. It was a little after ten and I was already in my sleeping-bag. I think that I was vaguely listening to the music from the pop club or whatever it is they have in the Barn when I heard voices close at hand. I looked through the tent flap and saw a man and a girl walking along the track in the direction of the farm.

'The man said, "I'd have to be still wet behind the ears to fall for that one, it's the oldest trick in the book!"

'Then the girl spoke for some time but more

quietly so that I could not hear what she said.

'When the man answered he sounded more reasonable. He said, "That's up to you, Sylvie. If it's a question of money . . ." But the girl interrupted, angrily. She said something about not wanting his money and she sounded as though she were crying.

'The man spoke to her soothingly. "Surely, Sylvie, you must have known the score?" ' Swann broke off. 'I didn't hear any more. I'm sure I've got the sense right in what I've told you but I couldn't swear to the exact words. I hope I haven't wasted your time.'

Wycliffe thanked him and told him that it would be necessary for him to put all that he had said into a formal statement. 'It might help us a great deal.' He hoped that he meant help, not confuse.

Sir John was still the perfect host. He even accompanied Wycliffe to the gates and stood, watching, while he walked the length of the quay to the steps. John Jenkins was there. So were the old men but the donkey had gone.

'Have you been waiting all this time?'

'No, Sir John told me when to pick you up.'

A well organized exercise! Wycliffe was piqued but his mood failed to survive the trip back. After all, he now had firm evidence that Peters had been with Sylvie an hour or so before she died.

It was as they were entering the harbour that he remembered with a twinge of conscience that it was the day of Sylvie's funeral. He had remarked on the number of boats at their moorings and John Jenkins had told him that afternoon trips had been cancelled because of the funeral. As the launch glided almost silently between the maze of craft he could see the hearse emerging from Bethel Street on to the quay.

In the islands funerals are still public occasions for the expression of communal concern and responsibility. There is no question of hustling the corpse off at thirty or forty miles an hour to the grave yard or the crematorium. It is paraded in stately progress through the streets with half the population following.

Wycliffe reached the top of the steps and mingled with the groups of tourists who, deprived of their planned enjoyment, were prepared to make do with what offered. Some of them were taking photographs. After all, it was the funeral of the murdered girl. As with all island funerals it was a men-only occasion and though they walked in threes behind the hearse, the procession stretched almost the length of the quay. Many of the men were in the clothes of their trade – blue jerseys and caps – with the addition of a black armband. The middle man of each group of three carried a wreath.

Charlie Martin was right up in front with the girl's father and, to Wycliffe's surprise, so was Jackie. He wore a dark suit and he looked so pale it seemed doubtful if he could complete the course. Jordan was well up in the procession with his two colleagues and so was the squint-eyed Ernie. But Peters had, presumably, decided that discretion was the better part or, maybe, funerals were not his thing.

It was strange and touching to see the solemn procession passing under the flowered arches which had been put up for the carnival events. Wycliffe wondered a little that they had not been cancelled for the night of the funeral but in this he showed lack of understanding for in a properly integrated society there is a time and place for everything.

After the procession had passed he climbed the slope to the school. Gill was there and he had had the good sense to send a wreath.

When Gill heard the new evidence he chuckled. 'Like the man said, it's the oldest trick in the book. The little dolly can't get her man any other way so she fixes it so that he puts her in the club. Somebody should have told her that it don't work any more in this wicked world.'

Wycliffe wondered what Sir John would have made of Gill.

'At least it proves Peters was lying and, incidentally, that Marsden wasn't.'

Wycliffe nodded. 'But I doubt if it gets us anywhere.'

Inspector Golly, who had listened with attention, preened his moustache with a careful forefinger. 'In spite of what Mr Gill says I would have thought that the girl's pregnancy gave Peters quite a strong motive.'

'How come?' From Gill.

'Because if the girl made a . . .'

'Stink?' Gill suggested.

'. . . a fuss, Peters' position on the island would have become untenable. He would have had to leave.'

They were interrupted by the telephone ringing. Wycliffe spoke to the duty-officer.

'DC Norris has just come in, sir. He thinks he's found the weapon.'

'I'll come out.'

The three men went out into the hall. Detective Constable Norris, a young, blond giant, was standing over his find which lay in a polythene bag on the duty-officer's desk. It was a five eighth diameter ring-bolt, that is to say, an iron rod, five eighths of an inch in diameter, with a ring at one end and threaded for a nut at the other. It was approximately eighteen inches long and heavily corroded. Scores of rust fragments lay loose in the bag.

'You can't see through the polythene very well, sir, but the ring end is encrusted with what looks like blood and other matter. There are also two tiny threads of material caught in a particularly rusty patch about halfway along the shank.'

Wycliffe turned to Gill. 'Have Scales examine it for prints – not that he will find any on that. After he's finished, send it to Franks. Then find out what Martin and Peters wore on Saturday night and get their outside clothing. Be as diplomatic as you like but get it and send it to forensic. Norris's threads may check or there may be fragments of rust or rust marks. It's worth a try.'

The constable had found the bolt on the quarry floor, twenty feet beyond where Sylvie's body was found. It was almost under a derelict tip-waggon, beyond the water which covered part of the quarry floor and largely sheltered from the rain by the waggon.

'He must have pitched it away, sir.'

Wycliffe agreed. 'Well, he wouldn't want to take it home with him, would he? I think I'll have another chat with Mr Peters.'

* * *

Usually Vince looked forward to Clarissa's shopping expeditions to the mainland. He could persuade himself that it would be pleasant to have the place to himself; a change, a holiday. There was another reason, he depended on her so completely that he felt the need, from time to time, to prove to himself that he could manage without her. But the truth always caught up with him before she had been gone more than a couple of hours. At first he would enjoy a refreshing sense of freedom, like a small boy let out of school, he would potter about, feed the cats, fetch the milk from the farm, plan his lunch and set about getting it. But by eleven or half-past he would be wondering about her, then worrying. If that damned helicopter came down into the sea . . . That would be the ultimate irony, then he would be left alone. It was absurd, of course, but it made him nervous. He would be sure to listen to the lunch-time news.

It was as though he were separated from a part of himself. Did that mean that he loved her? Did need equal love? He supposed that it was a kind of love, the love of a child for its mother, of an old woman for her dutiful daughter, selfish and born of necessity. That morning, when she was leaving, while she was raising her lips to him to be kissed, she was feeling in the pocket of his jacket to make sure that he had his tablets. The right pocket, he could no longer use the other. His left arm was rigid and useless, locked at the elbow, slightly bent.

'You'll be all right? You're sure?' There was a new intensity in her concern.

A mother rather than a mistress. And when he had other women she showed no jealousy, only concern

– concern for him. Her every act seemed to be tailored to his needs, even, he suspected, these periodic visits to the mainland when he could be alone for a little while and feel independent. It was good for him.

He took trouble over preparing his lunch then dawdled over eating it – killing time. Afterwards he allowed himself a thimbleful of brandy. At two o'clock he washed up and put the dishes away. It was very odd. On other days, when Clarissa was at home he could shut himself in his room for hours at a time, working on his flies, forgetful of himself. With Clarissa away he seemed to be fighting a running battle to keep his mind from introspection and self-pity.

Half past two. An hour before Roger was due. He wished that he had asked him to come earlier. He was tempted to go for a walk but refused to give way to weakness. He went upstairs to his room. His heart thumped unpleasantly as he climbed the stairs. Perhaps that was the brandy. He sat at his desk. The perpetual calendar said Wednesday 25 August. Clarissa had changed it that morning as she always did. In three days he would be twenty-nine years old.

Barbellion had lived to be thirty.

A year ago his doctor had recommended him to read Barbellion's *Journal of a Disappointed Man*. It had become his bible. He could recite long passages and often did so when he needed something to bolster his spirits. Barbellion had not conquered illness and death, he had civilized them and transformed them into a literary experience.

'I suppose the truth is I am at last broken in to the idea of death. Once it terrified me and once I hated it. But now it only annoys me . . . What embitters me is the humiliation of having to die . . . To think that the women I have loved will be marrying and forget, and that the men I have hated will continue on their way and forget I ever hated them – the ignominy of being dead!'

But Barbellion had been untroubled by guilt. Resentment, bitterness and frustration, but not guilt.

Recently he had been conscious of a growing sense of guilt, something which had not troubled him since adolescence. He supposed that it might be a morbid effect of his complaint but that did not help. He had reason to feel guilty.

He was troubled by an increasing desire to put himself right with the world. There were reparations which could be made and others which could not. He was glad that he had asked Roger to come.

Roger and Clarissa. But what about Sylvie?

And Jackie Martin. Last night he had been able to watch him with an interested detachment. There was something fundamentally childish about Jackie. The Peter Pan syndrome. A tragedy masquerading as a fairy tale.

He had once known and become close friends with a dwarf. At first it had been disconcerting, embarrassing, to hear him talking, expressing the opinions and sentiments of a mature man yet looking like a precocious child. He had similar feelings when he was with Jackie but for opposite reasons.

He wondered what Jackie would do – probably nothing.

He heard a noise downstairs. Roger must be early.

So, in the late afternoon, Wycliffe walked under the flowered arches by the harbour. Now elaborately decorated floats were parked in a long line. All the lorries in the island, carts towed by tractors, and a great variety of handcarts, prams, barrows and trolleys were all carrying large, unstable superstructures the skeletal elements of which were smothered with bunting, leaves and flowers. In the interests of business, carnival week started on a Wednesday so that its benefits were spread over two weeks' ration of visitors instead of one. Tonight the grand procession would be headed by the Lord Warden himself.

Wycliffe made his way up the hill out of the town. He had no special reason for going to see Peters himself, but he was attracted to the valley. Its mysterious isolation at the still centre of the island appealed to him.

It was hot in the afternoon sun. The pleasure boats had been to collect the trippers they had taken to the off-islands in the morning and they were on their way back, creeping across the great expanse of sea, each leaving a thin line of white wake, converging on the harbour. In the hotels and boarding houses they were preparing the evening meal but the beaches were still dotted with picnicking groups and children still shouted, screamed and splashed in the shallows. But the valley, when he came to the top of the steep slope, was deserted, the one place in the island where it was possible to forget that it *was* an island. Not, of course, what the tourist paid for.

Wycliffe walked down the stony path, crossed the bridge and entered the courtyard where the cats lay in the dappled shade of the pine tree. The air was heavy with its resinous scent.

A girl came running out of the house and collided with him. He caught and held her arms and she looked up at him with wide, frightened eyes. It was the girl from the pottery and the fear changed to relief as she recognized him. 'It's Vince, I think he must be dead!'

He followed her into the house but she stopped short in the hall. 'Upstairs.'

Wycliffe went upstairs. On the landing there were several doors but one stood open into a room furnished as an office or study. Peters was seated at a desk by the window, his body slumped forward. The glass of the lower window pane was shattered. There were a few slivers of glass on the desk but most of it must have fallen outside.

There could be no doubt that Peters was dead. A neat, round hole just forward of the left temple marked the entry of the bullet and, by bending over the body, he could see the ragged wound of exit behind the right ear, almost hidden by the position of the head on the desk. There was a little but not much blood.

Automatically his mind reconstructed the trajectory of the bullet. It seemed that the line of fire had been at a downward angle passing through the head from the left temple to the right tympanic bulla and out through the glass of the window. Passage through the bones of the skull must have given it sufficient wobble to shatter rather than pierce the glass.

The room was at the back of the house, overlooking the meadow with its pine trees and the row of beehives. Through a gap in the trees he could trace the course of the valley to a triangle of sea which glittered brilliantly in the sunshine.

The girl was waiting for him in the hall. She was nervous but not hysterical. 'He's dead, isn't he?'

'Yes. Where is Clarissa?'

She was dulled by the shock and it took her a moment to grasp the question. 'She's not back yet.'

'Back from where?'

She swept her hair from her face as though in an effort to clear her mind. 'Clarissa caught the morning flight to do some shopping on the mainland and she's due back at nine o'clock.' Her features wrinkled and she might have cried but she controlled herself. 'Somebody will have to tell her.'

Wycliffe was at the telephone which stood on a small table in the hall. He wiggled the receiver rest to attract the attention of the operator. 'Two-three-two, please.' It was the number allocated to his temporary headquarters. He was connected promptly and the duty-officer put him through to Chief Inspector Gill.

'Jimmy? I want you out here with the team . . . Yes, Peters . . . Shot. You might find out if Franks is still on the island, if not he'll have to come back. If you can't get hold of Franks, Ross is the local man.'

While they waited he asked the girl questions to keep her mind off the body upstairs. He realized that he did not even know her name.

'Luke – Brenda Luke.'

'Where do you live?'

'The Terrace.'

'With your parents?'

'With my mother. She's a widow.'

'What time did you arrive here?'

She glanced at her watch. 'About half-past four.'

'Did you see anybody?'

'No.'

'You went straight to the pottery?'

'I always do.'

'What made you come to the house just now?'

'The loo . . .'

'The front door was open?'

'Yes, it usually is in fine weather.' Her expression changed.

'What's the matter?'

'I've just remembered something.' She looked puzzled. 'When I came through the front door I heard somebody in the kitchen. I thought it was Vince and I called out as usual, "It's only me!" There was no answer but I didn't take any notice because they often don't hear or don't bother to answer.'

'But you are sure that you heard someone there?'

'Quite sure.'

Wycliffe left her to make a quick tour of the back of the house – kitchen, dining-room, sitting-room; there was no-one. The rooms were scrupulously tidy, nothing had been disturbed. He returned to the girl. 'What made you think that the noise you heard came from the kitchen?'

She frowned. 'I don't know – yes I do! It was

running water – a tap turned on and I think I heard the clink of glass as though somebody was washing up.'

'What about the woman who comes to do the cleaning?'

'Wednesday is her day off.'

Wycliffe went to the telephone once more and gave instructions for as many men as could be spared to cover the ground between the town and Salubrious Place, identifying everyone they met. There would be very few, the odd walker, birdwatcher or botanist, perhaps a couple looking for a quiet spot. It was a slim chance but one he dared not neglect.

The girl looked surprised and it seemed to worry her. 'Why did you do that?'

'We ought to find out who was about the place oughtn't we?'

She agreed, dubiously. 'I suppose so.'

Wycliffe changed the subject. 'Isn't it odd that Clarissa chose to go shopping on the woman's day off?'

Brenda smiled faintly. 'It was the only day Vince would let her go, he couldn't stand Nellie.'

'Nellie?'

'Nellie Martin – the daily help. She's all right really but Vince has got a thing about her.' Her face clouded. 'I keep talking about him as though he were still alive.'

'Nellie Martin – any relation to the other Martins I know?'

She looked surprised. Always having to remind herself that he knew nothing of her island. 'She's Jackie's mother!'

Another link.

They moved out of the hall and into the courtyard. She looked back at the square, grey-stone house, stark and sombre even in the sunshine. 'I didn't think he would really do it.'

'Do what?'

She was impatient. 'Kill himself. Clarissa thought he might, I know. Sometimes she was afraid to leave him alone and I used to tease her about it. But she was right, wasn't she?'

'What made her worry?' Wycliffe did not want to tell her at this stage that Peters had been murdered. 'Did he threaten to kill himself?'

She frowned. 'No, I don't think so but he got very depressed sometimes. It used to come over him suddenly and he would shut himself up in his room for hours at a time.' Brenda was coming to terms with the new tragedy and shock in the way most of us do, by discussing, explaining, rationalizing.

And Wycliffe encouraged her. 'What made him so depressed?'

She looked at him almost challengingly. 'People will say that he killed himself because he murdered Sylvie.'

'Is that what you think?'

'No. Vince had his faults, he was selfish but he wasn't like that. He wouldn't hurt anybody – not physically. In any case he had these fits of depression from the time he first came here. I think he was worried about something – something he wouldn't talk about. Sometimes, when he was talking to you, you would see a sudden change in him . . .'

'A change?'

She nodded. 'As though he had remembered something he was trying hard to forget.'

They were interrupted by the sound of a car engine. The police Land-Rover came into view at the top of the slope across the valley. The unsurfaced track was like a scree and the police driver took it with extreme caution.

'Did Peters have a gun?'

She shook her head. 'I don't know but I suppose he must have had.'

Chapter Six

The truck came to a halt on the far side of the bridge and Chief Inspector Gill got out, followed by Franks, two detectives and a constable in uniform. Franks crossed the bridge, beaming.

'Well, what have you got for me this time?' Nothing could daunt the chubby little doctor. He accepted death as others accept bills, unpleasant but inevitable. 'The first qualification for medicine,' he was fond of saying, 'is a total lack of imagination.'

Wycliffe greeted Gill while Detective Sergeant Smith, the squad's photographer, unloaded his equipment from the truck and draped it round the constable. Smith was a prematurely wizened dyspeptic who sucked soda mints most of the time. He scowled at Wycliffe and shambled off to the house followed by the constable. Roger Scales, whose speciality was fingerprints, came across the bridge carrying his little leather case. In contrast to Smith, with his little toothbrush moustache and his natty, gent's suiting he looked more like a prosperous accountant than a detective. But they were two of the hand-picked men in Wycliffe's squad and they had worked with him ever since his arrival in the West Country.

An hour and a half later Smith had added a score

of photographs of Peters dead to the thousands which must exist of Peters living. He had also photographed the room from every angle and in painstaking detail. Scales was at work on prints, many of them were photographed by Smith directly, others which were inaccessible to the camera had to be 'lifted' on tape, a tedious and highly skilled operation. Routine – and most of it, perhaps all of it, would prove to be a waste of time. But detectives, like archaeologists, rarely have a second chance to gather their data.

Franks had made a preliminary examination of the body, all he could do until it had been moved to the mortuary. Down in the hall four men smoked and chatted round the 'shell' which would be Peters' temporary coffin. They were waiting for Wycliffe to give the word for him to be moved. Franks made a final note in his tiny, gilt-edged notebook and snapped it shut.

'Ready, if you are.'

Wycliffe went to the top of the stairs and called to the men below. 'All right, boys!' He stood with Franks on the landing while the body was removed.

Franks was thoughtful. 'What do you make of it?'

'Why ask me?'

'You saw the powder marks?'

'I saw them.'

There had been scarcely any blackening of the skin but close examination had shown the presence of a scattering of colourless grains around the wound of entry. This meant that the shot had probably been fired from a distance of not more than two feet.

'You would have expected him to get up or

something, not to just sit there, waiting for it. Perhaps he thought it was a joke.'

'Evidently, it wasn't.'

'It must have been somebody he knew pretty well.'

'I agree, it's not common to be shot by a complete stranger.' Wycliffe was being deliberately uncommunicative – not because he wanted to snub Franks but in self defence. Talking tended to crystallize ideas and he wanted his thoughts to remain fluid. 'What we have to do is to find the gun.'

They followed the coffin downstairs and in the hall they were joined by Gill. The three of them went out into the sunshine. Wycliffe put a match to a half-smoked pipe, Jimmy Gill lit one of his cheroots which he hoped were less lethal than cigarettes. Franks mopped his bald head with a whiter-than-white handkerchief.

They walked across to the shade of the pine tree and Gill sat himself astride one of the metal chairs. 'Three of the divisional boys turned up – said they'd been told to cover the ground between here and town . . .'

'That's right. Did they meet anybody?'

'An octogenarian bird-watcher and a couple of teenagers who wanted to be alone. What's it about?'

Wycliffe was snappish. 'Never mind that now, Jimmy, you can find them something useful to do.'

Gill blew a cloud of smoke up into the pine tree. 'I have, they're gardening.'

'Gardening?'

'Looking for the bullet in the back meadow.'

Wycliffe sat on one of the chairs and Franks, after

flicking his handkerchief over another, sat down gingerly. 'This is a very nice place. One could do a lot worse than retire to a property like this. I wonder what he gave for it . . .'

'His life, by the look of it,' Gill said. He looked round disparagingly. 'It would give me the screaming abdabs in a week.'

'In my view,'. Franks said, pedantically, 'it must have been somebody he knew and trusted, not someone he would expect to shoot him.'

'I don't expect anybody to shoot me,' Wycliffe remarked, reasonably.

'But you know what I mean. To allow somebody to point a gun at you from a couple of feet and simply sit and wait for it . . .'

This line of thought had to be explained to Gill who was leaning back in his chair trying to blow smoke-rings.

'What bothers me is that he didn't leave the gun behind.'

'I don't see why that should bother you, he probably slung it away to make sure it couldn't be found and traced.'

'If I could be sure of that I'd feel a lot happier,' Wycliffe said.

'Me too!'

Franks looked from one to the other, mystified. Jimmy Gill explained. 'Nobody holds on to a hot gun unless they intend to use it again.'

'How long has he been dead?' Wycliffe demanded.

Franks considered, fingering the creases in his fine, herring-bone tweed. 'You know it's damn' difficult to give a straight answer. There were signs which bothered me. I don't want to say too much until I've had the chance . . .'

'An informed guess.'

Franks continued to prevaricate. 'Fully clothed, in a warm room . . . heat loss would be slow . . . The corneae were opaque but the lids being open . . .'

'Skip the pathology lesson, for God's sake!'

Franks grinned. 'On the evidence, so far, I'd say he died between half past three and four but I might have to revise that significantly. Anyway, not later than half past four.'

Wycliffe frowned. 'The girl who found him at a few minutes after five says she heard somebody in the kitchen . . .'

'Then if that somebody was the killer he must have hung round for at least half an hour after committing his crime.'

'What sort of idiot would do that?' Gill demanded.

'Perhaps he was looking for something,' Franks suggested.

'There were no signs of the place having been turned over.'

Wycliffe was staring absently into the bowl of his pipe which had gone out. 'The point is that we've got two murders on our hands. Are we to regard them as two cases or one?'

Gill, his long body contorted on the tiny chair, shifted impatiently. 'They must be one case. On an island this size you don't get two unrelated killings in a single week! In any case, whether he killed the girl or not, Peters was closely involved with her.'

Wycliffe nodded. 'I agree, so the question becomes, are we looking for two murderers or one?'

Ants were dropping from the branches of the pine tree and Franks was picking them off his suit with apparent concentration but he was following the discussion. 'Surely, if there are two murderers there must be two cases?'

'No, I get Mr Wycliffe's point. If Peters murdered the girl then someone – her father, for example, might have decided to settle accounts with Peters himself. After all, it was to deal with the possibility of such a vendetta situation that you were called in, wasn't it?'

Wycliffe knocked out his pipe on the heel of his shoe and started to refill it. 'I suppose you could put it that way though nobody anticipated murder. There are some big fish interested in this little pond and authority is very sensitive to public opinion in the islands. My inquiry was to be prophylactic rather than remedial. Nobody wanted a regular campaign to oust Peters. It would have got into the papers.'

Gill succeeded in blowing a smoke-ring and watched it rise in the still air until it disappeared in the branches of the tree. 'All the same, Sylvie was murdered, and now Peters.'

Wycliffe stood up, his hands thrust deep into his coat pockets. He said, almost apologetically, 'Peters died because Sylvie died, but why?'

It was a rhetorical question or, rather, it was a question that he was asking himself. He stood, apparently undecided what to do. 'Sylvie's funeral was this afternoon.'

'So?' Gill looked at him with curiosity.

'There must be quite a few people with alibis for this. I got back at half past two and the funeral was then on its way to the cemetery. I imagine there was some sort of do afterwards – or wasn't there?'

Gill nodded, thoughtfully. 'There was, at Charlie's place. I'll look into it.'

Wycliffe still stood, irresolute. 'I think I'll take a look round.' He set off across the courtyard in the direction of the house but after a few steps he turned round. 'What happened to Brenda Luke?'

'I sent her home with Jordan. I told her we would talk to her later.'

Wycliffe said nothing and continued on his way to the house, head bent, shoulders drooping.

Franks looked after him with concern. 'What's the matter with him? He doesn't seem to be his usual self.'

Gill grimaced. 'He feels responsible for Peters.' He threw the butt-end of his cheroot in the direction of a sleeping cat and missed. 'I'd rather have an ulcer than a bloody conscience.'

In the hall Wycliffe met Sergeant Scales, his fingerprint man. Scales was the sort to get through a lot of work without flapping. 'We've finished his room, sir, and we've started down here. Peters' own prints, of course, are all over the place upstairs. And there are two female sets which occur several times; I assume they belong to his mistress and the cleaning woman. Then there is a single set – all four fingers of the right hand – a man's, quite clear and definite and fresh. They are on the side of the filing cabinet, near the top edge, as though somebody had rested against the cabinet, his arm on the top, his fingers bent over the edge.'

'Made today?'

'I think so. I would be surprised if they were older but I could be wrong.'

'What about the gun?'

'No sign of it yet but one of the divisional men found an unopened box of .38 revolver ammunition in that drawer.' He pointed to one of the top drawers of a chest of drawers which stood in the hall.

'Unopened?'

'That's right, sir. Makes you think doesn't it?'

'It does indeed. Anybody upstairs?'

'Not at the moment, sir. Andrews and Cole will be starting their inventory directly.'

Wycliffe went upstairs and shut himself in the dead man's room. He closed the door with a satisfaction he would have found difficult to explain. He wanted to immerse himself in the world of the dead man, to exclude comment, suggestion and discussion. Above all he did not want to be watched.

Although Scales and Smith had gone over the room with meticulous thoroughness he knew that they would have been scrupulously careful to put everything back as they had found it. Apart from any changes the murderer had made the room was as it had been when Peters sat in his chair that afternoon . . . doing what? The desktop was bare except for a telephone, a pen tray, a blank scribbling pad and a calendar. The pen tray held an expensive ball-point and a gold fountain pen engraved 'V.P.'.

When does a man sit at his desk with nothing in front of him? When he is bored, when he wants to think. Wycliffe started to pry into the desk drawers. Soon two detectives would be busy making a detailed inventory of everything in the room and, eventually, he would be presented with several pages of typescript itemizing the contents of every drawer and cupboard. All the same he couldn't resist poking about for himself. There was nothing of interest in the desk – stationery, a few bills, a couple of snapshots of Clarissa and the usual collection of rubbish most people hoard in drawers. Several keys without identification labels.

Wycliffe got up and started to prowl about the room. The insect cabinet consisted of a score of glass-topped, cork-lined drawers, each drawer contained hundreds of flies and each fly was spread-eagled on a pin with a little white card giving coded information about it. On the top of the cabinet a card index file contained the records in Peters' spidery hand.

There were sounds of heavy footsteps on the stairs, a peremptory knock and a head round the door. 'If it's convenient to start the inventory, sir . . .'

'It isn't, laddie! Go away.'

The big filing cabinet was divided into two parts, one part held correspondence, mainly, it seemed, with his accountant and various agents; the rest of the cabinet – nine or ten drawers – was filled with press cuttings, photographs, hand-outs and hundreds of record sleeves from recording companies all over the world.

The book shelves held mainly works on entomology, flies in particular, but there were a number of books on medical subjects, a few of them professional texts, most of the 'health for all' variety. Was Peters a hypochondriac?

The built-in cupboard contained an expensive

looking binocular microscope, a few bits of scientific apparatus which Wycliffe could not identify and a deed-box which was locked. He found the key among those in the desk drawer.

The box contained a bundle of manilla folders, each one labelled with the title of a song. Wycliffe recognized several of Peters' hits. Each folder held in its pocket a small tape, presumably a recording of the song, and a lyric, written in a neat schoolboy hand and corrected with scratchings out and interpolations. Altogether they made an unpretentious little bundle but the contents of the box had made several fortunes.

He re-locked the box and put the key back in the desk drawer.

Although he would never admit it, Wycliffe rather liked poking about in somebody else's room. It was all part of his intense interest in people. Some men spend their days watching birds or badgers or red deer, Wycliffe watched people. His interest was usually sympathetic, never malicious, and what he learned, not only helped him with his job but helped him to come to terms with himself. He went back to the chair by the window, the chair in which Peters had died, and sat, staring out into the meadow. After a little while his mind was almost a total blank. Was this how Peters had been when his killer arrived? Had he been slow to react because he was deep in a mindless reverie?

This room probably had more in it of the man Peters than any other place. Wycliffe was sitting in Peters' chair, surrounded by Peters' belongings. Apart from the chalk circles marking prints the room was as Peters had made it, as he had lived in it.

But it did not help him to form a clear picture of the man. Peters remained an enigma. A clever boy, son of a working-class family. 'O' levels, 'A' levels, University. But he throws up a promising academic career for the 'Scene'. Nothing remarkable about that. More remarkable, he had made it to the top. Fame and fortune, girls and girls. Then he chucks it in. Why? Disgust? Disillusionment? If so, would he have treasured all these mementoes of those years? Here in this room were the props of Vince, the Pop Idol, cheek by jowl with the trappings of Peters, the student. There seemed to be a fundamental ambivalence at the core of his life.

Wycliffe got up from his chair and went out on to the landing where Andrews and Cole were waiting to start their inventory. 'It's all yours.'

He was uneasy. He felt that he had achieved nothing but that he had come close to making a real step forward. He had missed something obvious, perhaps failed to interpret evidence which had been presented to him.

Preoccupied and morose he was driven back to town by a uniformed constable.

The quay was alive with people, the carnival procession had formed up, the band was playing and they were about to move off on their tour of the town. He told his driver to drop him at the Tower House and to take the car back through the side streets. He felt sure that Nellie Martin would not be watching the procession.

She answered his knock. 'You again! What is it now? My son is out.'

'I wanted to talk to you, Mrs Martin.'

Reluctantly she stood aside and after she had closed the door she followed him into their living-room which was also the kitchen. The old man was seated in his chair by the stove, his head lolled back, his eyes were closed and a weak, bubbling sound came from his open mouth. Wycliffe had never seen a living person so white, even his lips were no more than a pinkish margin to the mouth.

'You haven't been to the Peters' place today?'

'It's my day off.'

'I'm afraid I have some bad news for you. Mr Peters is dead.'

A kettle on the stove had started to boil and she moved it away from the heat. She had not asked him to sit down but he did so, on a heavy, dining chair with a fretted back and upholstered seat. There was not a scrap of comfort anywhere in the room.

'He was shot.'

'You mean he committed suicide?'

'He was murdered.'

She gave no sign of surprise or interest.

'Do you know if Peters owned a gun?'

'He had a gun – yes.'

'How do you know?'

'I clean the place, don't I? Anyway he made no secret of it, he kept it in one of the drawers of the chest in the hall.'

'Has he ever mentioned it to you?'

'When I first went there to work he used it once or twice to fire at a target in the meadow but he gave that up.'

'Why?'

She shrugged. 'How should I know?'

The band was passing outside the window and conversation became impossible but the old man slept on undisturbed. The window was tight shut and with the stove burning the heat in the room was unbearable.

'Was there ammunition in the drawer with the gun?'

'There was a box, I suppose it was ammunition, I didn't take much notice.'

'One box or two?'

She shook her head. 'I couldn't say. I've got other things to think about.'

'Working in the house as you did you must know something of his affairs. Would you say that there was anybody with whom he was on particularly bad terms?'

A bitter little smile. 'Just about everybody on the island.'

'You know exactly what I mean, Mrs Martin.'

She was brushing ash out of the fender. She seemed quite incapable of standing still and most of the time she had her back to him. Now she turned on him. 'And what if I do? It's none of my business!'

'Murder is everybody's business.' The hoary old platitude but he had to say something.

Through the lace blinds he could see vague outlines of the decorated floats passing by and there was frequent clapping and mild cheering. They could even hear the money boxes of the collectors being rattled under the noses of the spectators.

'There was his brother.'

'Roger?'

She nodded. 'Always falling out over money. No love lost between them two.' It was obvious that she had more to tell but by pressing her he might get less than by letting her go her own way. In due course it came.

'I heard him on the telephone yesterday.'

'To Roger?'

'They had an appointment for this afternoon – he asked him to come to the house. Between half past three and four, he said.'

'You are sure of that?'

'I said it, didn't I?'

'Are you willing to put what you have said into a statement and sign it?'

'If I have to.'

As he was leaving she volunteered one more piece of information. 'You know where to find him I suppose?'

'I understand that he lodges at the Quay Café.'

'You could call it that.'

He was glad to get out on to the quay in the fresh air. There was nobody about but he could hear the band playing somewhere in the town. He noticed that the set pieces for the night's firework display had been erected on rafts in the harbour.

Back at his headquarters Inspector Golly was waiting for him and followed him into his office. 'After the funeral . . .'

'One moment, Mr Golly. Who's on duty?'

'Sergeant Scales and one of the local men, PC Trembath.'

Wycliffe picked up the telephone and asked for Trembath to be sent in. The young man arrived promptly, anxious to make a good impression.

'You know Roger Peters?'

'Yes, sir.'

'I want you to write out his description, give it to Mr Golly and he will see that it is circulated to all our men.'

'You want him brought in, sir?' Golly enquired.

'I do. For questioning. And Trembath – I want you, after you've written the description, to go home and change into plain clothes. Then go to the Quay Café and if Peters is not there wait for him. Don't leave until you are relieved or until you bring Peters in.'

When Trembath had gone Wycliffe turned to Golly. 'Now, about the funeral . . .'

Golly had a list of those who had returned to Charlie Martin's house after the funeral. There were between thirty and forty names and among them Wycliffe noted Sylvie's father and Jackie Martin.

'As far as can be ascertained, sir, all these men were there until at least four o'clock.'

'Which makes a pretty good alibi for quite a few. I want this list checked and cross-checked, Mr Golly. And don't forget, nobody is going to be anxious to help.'

A quarter past eight. Time to pick up Brenda Luke and take her to the airport. He had had nothing to eat since lunchtime but he was anxious to see for himself how Clarissa received the news of Peters' death.

In Jordan's little car he drove through the town and up a steep hill to The Terrace where the Lukes lived. The streets were clear for the carnival procession had reached the recreation ground from where they would disperse after judging.

Mrs Luke was outsize and addicted to floral voile dresses worn with ropes of imitation pearls draped over her bosom. Her hair, tinted with a mauve rinse, was set in unnatural waves and her heavily made-up lips were almost lost in the folds of fat which encroached from either side. 'I don't want to be rude but I was just going out again, another minute and you would have missed me altogether!' Her manner was arch, as though they shared a salacious secret. 'Never mind! It's Brenda you've come to see, isn't it?'

Wycliffe was shown into a tiny sitting-room in which there was scarcely space for the three-piece suite.

'Brenda!'

Brenda came in looking pale.

'Now, you must tell her, Mr Wycliffe, not to worry. She's a great one for taking other people's troubles on her shoulders.' She looked at her daughter critically. 'Look at her! She looks quite peaky – you're not sickening for something are you?'

'She's had a shock, Mrs Luke, it's only natural that she should be upset – two of her friends in a few days . . .'

'Not friends exactly – acquaintances, you might say. I know it's sad, a tragedy really, but you can't live other people's lives for them – that's what I always say.' She looked from her daughter to Wycliffe and back again. 'Well, if that's all it is, I'll leave you to it.' She was on her way out into the passage when she turned back. 'Oh, Bren, I forgot.

You're too late to see the carnival but Mrs Paul asked me to come to their place to watch the fireworks. Why don't you come down later – when Mr Wycliffe has finished with you? It would cheer you up.'

'I'll think about it, mother.'

After a moment or two the front door slammed. Wycliffe wondered if Mr Luke had died in self defence. The girl looked at him with a vaguely apologetic look.

'I thought you might like to come to the airport with me to meet Clarissa. She has to be told.'

'You want me to tell her?'

'It might be better.'

She nodded. 'I think you're right.' She was a kindly, sensible girl.

'I've got a car outside.'

She fetched her coat and they got into the little blue and white Morris. Wycliffe drove inexpertly but slowly through the narrow lanes to the heliport. Brenda sat with her knees together, her skirt pulled down as far as it would go but still not far enough to cover her plump thighs. She seemed anxious to talk.

'I got to know Clarissa soon after they came here . . . I felt sorry for her really. I know Vince is dead but he wasn't fair to her.' She swept back the hair from her face in a quick movement. 'He was selfish – always thinking of himself . . . Anyway, she started the pottery. I think she wanted to feel a bit independent. I'd done some pottery at school and she said I had a flair . . . I started to help out when she got busy, then we came to an arrangement – commission. Another season and I'd probably have given up my job and gone to work there full time.'

'You have another job?'

She seemed surprised by his ignorance. 'I work for the Boat Syndicate, for Charlie Martin. Of course there isn't much to do in the winter but they're very good – always full pay. But it isn't much of a job – boring.' The ultimate condemnation.

All she needed was a gentle prod now and then to keep her going. 'Clarissa is sweet.'

'Did they quarrel?'

She shook her head. 'You couldn't quarrel with Clarissa – nobody could. As far as Vince was concerned, she just took what he dished out. No, he didn't ill-treat her – not hit her or anything like that. He just took notice of her when it suited him and ignored her at other times.'

Evidently she had not fallen for Peters like the others, or, if she had, disillusionment had followed.

'Did they have many visitors?'

'Visitors? Not very often. Apart from the kids, that is. And Jackie Martin, if you count him. Once in a while his accountant or his agent would come over, then, of course, there was his brother – Roger.'

'What about Roger?'

'He's older than Vince, some sort of salesman, I think, though he can't do very much work.'

'Does he come often?'

'He seems to spend most of his time on the island and he visits Vince pretty often. He seems to be short of money and I think he sponges on Vince.'

'When did you last see him at the house?'

She considered. 'Friday, I think it was – no, Thursday. They had a row.'

They had arrived at the heliport. Wycliffe parked

his car and they walked through the little waiting-room on to the grass landing field. The sun was dipping into the sea, that sad, solemn moment of a summer day when everything is suffused with golden light. Wycliffe recalled his youth. Chapel on Sunday evenings with the sun filtered through cheap stained glass. The sound of a brass band reached them from the town.

'They quarrelled?'

'Yes. Clarissa and I were working in the pottery and we went over to the house to get a drink. Roger was there and Vince was telling him off. He seemed quite worked up. Of course he stopped when we arrived and I didn't quite gather what it was about but afterwards Clarissa said, "I'm glad Vince is putting his foot down. Roger is very weak and he will live off Vince if he can." It was the most I've ever heard Clarissa say against anybody.'

She stared out over the glassy sea. 'I can see the helicopter.'

Then Wycliffe spotted it, a black dot creeping almost imperceptibly nearer. 'Is Roger married?'

'Separated.'

'Apparently he doesn't stay with Vince when he's here.'

She gave a quick, faint smile. 'No, he lodges at the café on the quay.'

'So?'

'The café is run by a widow woman – Wendy Hicks. The gossip is that Roger Peters is her lover.'

'Are there any other relatives?'

'No, Clarissa says both parents are dead and there were no other children.'

A moment while they watched the helicopter drawing nearer, seeming to move crabwise across the sky.

'Brenda, there's something I must tell you before Clarissa comes. Vince did not kill himself, he was murdered.'

She did not seem to be surprised. 'I wondered. When I thought it over it seemed odd that you were so anxious to find out who it was in the kitchen. Do you think it could have been . . . ?'

The beat of the rotor blades was suddenly very close, then overhead. The machine hovered like an angry mosquito then dropped quickly and smoothly to the ground. The engine cut and the blades came to rest.

'There she is.'

Wycliffe saw the slim, dark figure at the top of the steps, her arms full of parcels. She saw Brenda and tried to wave. Brenda went to meet her. He saw them meet and then he saw the vivacity die from Clarissa's face and a frightening blankness take its place. She released her parcels to Brenda mechanically and, mechanically, she allowed herself to be guided towards him.

'Oh, yes, the police.' Complete acceptance.

She sat beside him in the little car, her hands resting listlessly in her lap, her eyes looking straight ahead. He had to tell her that she could not go to Salubrious Place until his men had finished there. 'You'll be able to use at least part of the house tonight but wouldn't it be better if you stayed in the town?'

'I want to go home as soon as possible.' Tonelessly.

'I'll come with you, Clarissa, keep you company.'

'Thank you.'

'Meantime you must come home with me.'

Wycliffe was impressed by her grief. No demonstration. Many people are surprised and hurt when misfortune strikes home, others are always aware that it could happen. The world is divided into those who say, 'Not to me!' and the others who ask, 'Why not?'

'There are one or two questions I must ask you now,' Wycliffe said. 'The rest can wait.'

'I want to help.'

'Did Mr Peters own a gun?'

A faint, sad smile. 'Please call him Vince, never was he called Mr Peters. Yes, he had a gun. I do not know why. I think he bought it in America for fun. Once or twice, a long time ago, he played with it in the meadow – shooting at bottles, but I did not like that.'

'Where did he keep it?'

'In one of the drawers of the chest in the hall. I did not want it in the house but when I say that he just laugh at me.'

'Was there ammunition with the gun?'

'Yes, there were two boxes but one was not full – some had been used.'

'Who else knew of the gun?'

She frowned. 'I do not know. I do not think he told anyone and I did not. I would think no-one knew that it was there.'

'The cleaning woman?'

'Oh, yes, she would know, I suppose.'

'His brother?'

'Roger?' She hesitated. 'Roger might know that

Vince had a gun but I do not think he would know where it was kept.'

'Jackie Martin?'

She hesitated again. 'I do not think Jackie Martin would know unless his mother told him.'

Wycliffe thanked her. 'I won't trouble you any more tonight.' He promised that he would arrange transport for them to Salubrious Place when his men had finished. 'It may be late.'

Then he drove them in silence to the little terraced house above the town. The streets were mysterious in a purple summer dusk.

The town was empty, everybody was gathered on the quay to watch the fireworks. He threaded through narrow alleys to avoid the harbour and came out at the foot of the steep slope up to the school. As he parked the car in the playground there was a powerful hissing sound, a trail of fire across the sky, a loud report and a shower of stars crackling overhead. The first rocket.

The duty-officer sat by the radio panel. A detective was writing his report, it was quiet as a church. He went through to his office. Jimmy Gill was supervising the search at Salubrious Place.

Searching a house takes a long time when you have no idea what you are looking for and very little idea of what may turn out to be important when you find it.

Wycliffe filled his pipe, taking his time, lit it and puffed contentment. The firework display was reaching a climax. From his chair he could look down on the harbour. A set piece was spluttering and spitting fire on its floating raft. 'Welcome to the Islands', reflected faithfully in the oily black water. Peters might have doubted the sincerity of the greeting. For a guilty moment Wycliffe wished himself young again, a girl on his arm, embracing, kissing, whispering and losing identity in the crowd which was as good-natured as the warm darkness.

He sat a while watching the fireworks without switching on the lights. Then he reached for the telephone and asked to be connected to the hospital where the mortuary was and where Franks was conducting the post-mortem. He had to wait some time before they could get Franks on the line and when he came he sounded tired.

'I thought you would be watching the fireworks.'

'I am. Have you finished?'

'All I can do tonight.'

'One question – was Peters in good health?'

Franks laughed shortly. 'You noticed? I thought I had news for you.'

Wycliffe had noticed nothing physical to lead him to the conclusion that Peters was seriously ill. He had deduced illness from seemingly irreconcilable aspects of the young man's life.

'I wondered this afternoon,' Franks went on. 'His left arm was rigid. Of course, that could have been due to local injury, but it wasn't.'

'What was wrong with him?'

'Disseminated or multiple sclerosis. Small areas of the nervous system become sclerotized and these areas may be anywhere in the brain or spinal cord. The disease is progressive . . .'

'It's a death sentence, isn't it?'

'Not necessarily, by any means. Its progress may

be so slow that the expectation of life is scarcely affected.'

'But with Peters?'

'I've had a word with Ross who was his GP – a good chap. Ross was worried, there was no sign of a let-up.'

'How long would he have had?'

'Impossible to say, but if there was no slowing down it could hardly have been more than two or three years.'

So Peters had been under sentence.

'Did he know?'

'In general terms – yes. Ross said he took it very well. Usually people suffering from the disease are encouraged to carry on with their jobs but in his case . . . Well, co-ordination was the essence of it and that tends to suffer in the early stages.'

It helped to resolve the enigma and put a tragedy in its place.

A fusillade of rockets shot into the air, diverged and fell in cascades of crepitating stars.

'Would his mind have been affected?'

'How the hell would I know? It depends on the distribution of sclerotized areas.'

'What about his blood group?'

'Group "A".'

'So he could have been the child's father?'

'Yes.'

'Anything else for me?'

'Not much, the track of the bullet was just as it seemed to be – nothing fancy.'

'Time of death?'

'I've found nothing to make me change my mind.

Probably between three-thirty and four-thirty. I can't be more definite.'

'What about his clothing?'

'I didn't get anything from it but I've had it packed up ready for your people to collect. I suppose it will have to go to forensic?'

'I suppose so, but there's not much point.'

'I don't suppose you've had a chance to do anything with that ring bolt I sent you?'

Franks was smug. 'I made time. It's the weapon all right. Blood, a small amount of hair and tissue . . . It's her blood group and her hair.'

'How many blows with a thing like that?'

'Perhaps one, more likely two.'

'Thanks. Good night.'

Down at the harbour, another set piece. Catherine wheels, red, green and white, whirling in a frenzied pattern.

Multiple sclerosis. It explained a lot.

Wycliffe's thoughts ranged over the day which had started with his tentative, almost half-hearted investigation into the death of a young girl. Her death had been made to look like suicide – or accident. If it hadn't been for the islanders there would have been no awkward questions. She had been clubbed to death. Peters had been shot. Had they died by the same hand? Wycliffe's training would tell him that they had not. Case histories show that multiple killers stick to one method. They are poisoners, or stranglers, or knife men, or they bludgeon their victims to death. But the motives for such killings are usually pathological, that is to say, they are not 'reasonable' to the ordinary man. Is it likely that someone more rationally motivated might be less hidebound? More opportunist in his approach? Wycliffe was inclined to think so and for that reason he was unwilling to discount the possibility that there had been only one killer. On the other hand, he must consider the alternative.

Like every investigator, detective or scientist, Wycliffe had learned that the key to success lies in asking the right questions and the selection of the 'right' questions seems to be an intuitive process. At least he had never come across a set of rules for doing it.

Now he felt that the right question was 'Why?' not 'Who?' Why had Sylvie been bludgeoned? Why had Peters been shot? He was sure that the answers would be linked.

He resisted the temptation to try to answer his questions now. He had found it best not to strain too hard after truth. Better to let impressions, facts, ideas and incidents accumulate, mix and blend and crystallize in the slow chemistry of the mind.

Chapter Seven

He was restless. He telephoned Jimmy Gill who had no news for him. He arranged for one of Jimmy's team to fetch Clarissa from the Lukes' and bring her home. 'I expect that she will come back with the Luke girl. Let them carry on as normally as possible.'

Twenty minutes past ten. If he went back to the Jordans' he could hardly ask them to cook him a meal and he had no appetite for what he could expect from the canteen. He walked down the corridor to the operations room. The duty-officer was reading a newspaper, a cup of tea at his elbow. One of the divisional men was typing his report. More paper. Always more paper. It was a disease – Parkinson's disease. He chuckled at the bad pun.

'Good night, sergeant.'

'Good night, sir.'

And the same to you.

He strolled through the playground and down the slope to the quay. The fireworks were over and chains of fairy lights had been switched on. Scores of couples were shuffling round the wharf to waltz tunes played by the brass band who must have been almost blown out.

The Quay Café was one of the granite fronted houses facing the harbour. It had a shop front but the windows were covered with net curtains which made it difficult to see inside. He pushed open the door. Trembath was there and spotted him at once. A moment later they were resting with their arms on the quay wall, looking out over the harbour.

'So he's not turned up?'

'No, sir. At first she pretended she hadn't seen him since Monday but I wouldn't wear that and in the end she said he was out pollacking with the Rowses.'

'Is that likely?'

'Quite likely, sir. I know he often goes out with the Rowse brothers and there's plenty of pollack about at the moment.'

'Which means what?'

'That he might not be back until two or three in the morning.'

'What's the food like in there?'

'The food? All right, I suppose. Chips with everything.'

'You get along home. I expect you've got a wife waiting for you.'

'Yes, sir, but . . .'

'Scoot, laddie!'

He went across to the café.

A dozen marble-topped tables, a black and white tiled floor, a counter with tea and coffee machines and shelves with cakes and sandwiches on paper doilies. An ABC tearoom, 1992 vintage. But on the wall behind the counter there was a large mirror with the menu written on it in white water paint. As Trembath had said, chips with everything. A door in the back wall stood open and through it he could see the kitchen beyond and hear the voices of two women.

At one of the tables a boatman in his blue jersey and still wearing his cap, was eating forkfuls of beans and sausages washed down by gulps of strong tea. At another table a young couple sat with empty coffee cups in front of them. Wycliffe sensed that they were in the silent stage of a quarrel, looking at each other surreptitiously and wondering if it would be possible to make it up before they had to separate for the night.

One of the women came through from the kitchen. Thirty-four or five, not bad looking, plump, comfortable, but her face over-made-up. Her lips were slashes of crimson and her eyelids the colour of a ripe bruise. Her see-through blouse was well filled. She wiped the counter with a damp cloth and asked him what he wanted.

'Mrs Hicks?'

She nodded.

'Roger in?'

She was contemptuous. 'You know the answer to that one. I wasn't born yesterday.'

'I'll wait.'

She paused, as though considering. 'You'll have to wait a long time.'

'Until when?'

'Maybe all night.'

'Then I shall need something to eat. Say, eggs and sausages. No chips. And I'll start with some coffee.'

She nodded towards one of the tables. 'I'll bring it.'

A long wait.

It had been half past ten when he settled down to his meal. Soon afterwards the dancing on the quay had stopped and there was an influx of customers, mostly young people, presumably with good digestions. The widow and her unseen helper in the kitchen were kept busy. After his meal Wycliffe smoked his pipe and listened to the chatter at the tables. He heard no mention of Peters. Most of the customers seemed to be visitors and the news hadn't got round to them. He went out on to the wharf and sat on a bollard from where he could keep an eye on the café. The fairy lights made multicoloured streamers on the water. Along the quay, the Seymour Arms was a blaze of light and the noise of people all talking and shouting at once reached him as a pleasant murmur.

By half past eleven people were leaving the café and there were no new customers. He went back inside, the widow was putting chairs on some of the tables and there were only two customers left. She looked at him wearily. 'I thought you'd gone.'

He sat at his former table, now laden with dirty dishes. The two remaining customers paid their bill and left.

'I'm closing.'

He did not answer and she went over to the shop door and reversed the 'open' card.

'What do you want him for?'

'Just a few questions.'

She had finished putting up the chairs on the cleared tables, now she came and sat near him. 'God! I'm all in.' She put her feet on a second chair and leaned forward to massage her ankles.

Wycliffe smoked his pipe. 'Does he come here often?'

'Pretty often.'

'As a lodger?'

'You could say that.'

'You mean that he's more than a lodger?'

She lit a cigarette and puffed luxuriously. 'I mean that he doesn't pay his rent.' She grinned and added, 'All the same, he's good company and it's nice to have a man about the place again. I won't deny it.'

She seemed a decent body, the sort Wycliffe could get on with. A realist. She had life taped.

'Why don't you marry him?'

She looked at him speculatively. 'You're an odd sort of copper. As to marriage, I've got the café, what's he got?'

'A job, I suppose, and a brother with money.'

She laughed. 'His job doesn't amount to much. He's a freelance salesman working on commission and most weeks he doesn't make enough to live on. Poor old Rog couldn't sell nuts to a squirrel. As to his brother's money, if Roger ever got his hands on that I wouldn't see him for dust. I've got no illusions about Master Roger but beggars can't be choosers and I know where I am with him.'

'Where does he live when he's not here?'

'He's got a room in Plymouth – Frobisher Terrace.'

Wycliffe smoked placidly. The clock on the glass shelf above the sandwiches showed a quarter to twelve. A little old woman wearing a shabby brown coat down to her ankles came through the door from the kitchen. She clutched a paper carrier bag.

'I'll take the sandwiches.'

The widow sighed. 'You do that, Elsie, they won't be much by tomorrow.'

The old woman reached down the sandwiches, wrapped them in a couple of paper doilies and put them in her carrier bag. 'I'm off, then. I've finished most of the washing up but I'll do the rest in the morning.'

'All right, Elsie, thanks.'

The old woman trotted over to the door and let herself out. 'Good night, then!'

The widow watched her go. 'Poor old soul, she's got nobody. She comes here as much as anything for the company.' She got up and went behind the counter; when she came back she was carrying two bottles of ale and glasses. 'Drink?'

'Thanks.'

They sat opposite each other, drinking their beer.

'If you ask me, it's the chance of getting hold of his brother's money that ruined Roger.'

'Not much of a chance, surely.'

She wiped her lips with the back of her hand. 'I don't know about that. Vince could pop off at any time.'

'How do you know that?'

'Rog told me, he's got something wrong with his nerves. That's why he packed it in with the pop business.'

'Even so, there's no certainty that Roger would benefit, is there?'

'I don't know, but blood is thicker than water – at least, that's what they say.'

'Vince is dead.'

'Dead?' She put down her glass which had been

halfway to her lips. 'Is that why you're here? What's it got to do with the police?'

'He was shot.'

'You mean that he shot himself?'

'He was murdered.'

She kneaded her left breast unselfconsciously. 'You think Roger did it?'

'It's just one possibility.'

She did not argue. 'When did it happen?'

'This afternoon.'

'Then it couldn't have been Roger, he was over to Morvyl with Billy Rowse. The Rowses are mechanics and Billy had to go over to see to Sam Tripp's wind pump.'

'When did he get back?'

'About seven, I think it was.'

'And where is he now?'

She looked pained. 'I told Eddie Trembath, he's out pollacking with the Rowses.'

'On carnival night?'

She smiled wearily. 'That sort of thing doesn't mean much to the islanders, it's for the trade. When there's pollack about and the weather is fair you won't catch many of the menfolk gawping at processions and fireworks. A gallon of beer in the bottom of the boat and they're away.'

Wycliffe could sympathize.

She added, 'As I told you, he could be away all night, you'd much better leave it till morning.'

Wycliffe shook his head.

'All right, suit yourself.' She finished her beer and gathered up the empties and the glasses. 'I must get on.'

Wycliffe felt drowsy. For a time he was dimly aware of the widow woman moving around, clearing up, then there were gaps. He must have dozed fitfully. Two or three times he woke with a start to find her still carrying dishes into the kitchen or putting chairs on to tables, then, the next time, the café was empty, everything had been cleared away and the clock on the glass shelf showed a quarter past one.

He felt foolish and he had a headache. The kitchen was in darkness and he called out, 'Mrs Hicks!' Then he found the switch for the kitchen lights. 'Mrs Hicks! Are you there?' He found the stairs at the back of the kitchen and went up, wondering what he would do if she had gone to bed. A small landing with three doors opening off. He tried them all, flicking switches. Two bedrooms, unoccupied, and a long sitting-room at the front, overlooking the harbour.

For the first time he noticed that it was raining, streaming down the windows and he could hear water chuckling in the downpipe. He went back downstairs feeling a fool. As he entered the café, the shop door opened and the widow came in. She stood there, her plastic mackintosh dripping on to the floor, and she looked at him diffidently, a little frightened, like a naughty child who expects to be smacked. She opened her mouth to speak but he brushed past her, out into the rain.

'Take the umbrella! You'll get soaked!'

But his pride would not let him hear. Although he was not far from Jordan's house he was wet through before he got there. But he was beginning to recover his good humour, even to see the funny side. Although Peters had been tipped off by his widow woman, it was unlikely that he could get away from the islands.

From Jordan's office, with his clothes dripping on to the floor and forming a pool on the linoleum, he phoned his headquarters at the school and arranged for a watch to be kept on the café. Then he crept up to his room. From across the landing, Jordan's snoring continued without interruption.

Next morning it was still raining, the waterfront was deserted, the boats were still at their moorings and it looked as though they would stay there. He stopped at the shop to buy tobacco and a newspaper. From the rack, the tabloids bleated in heavy, black type:

VINCE PETERS DEAD

POP STAR FOUND DEAD

Wycliffe bought a *Guardian*; its pale-pink literacy appealed to him. No banner headlines; a three-column spread on the economic situation, but they still found space on the front page for a decorous headline in twenty-four-point:

MYSTERY DEATH OF FORMER POP STAR

The facts, as Wycliffe had made them known, were followed by a potted biography of Peters and, 'The police are treating Peters' death as murder. Detective Superintendent Wycliffe is investigating a possibility that Peters' death may be linked with that of a nineteen-year-old girl whose body was found in a disused quarry on the island last Sunday . . .'

Sylvie's death had made scarcely a ripple in Fleet Street but linked with the Peters shooting it would do better.

When he reached the school there had been no news of Roger Peters. The Rowse brothers had been summoned and were being questioned by Detective Sergeant Gifford, one of the divisional men. Wycliffe went along to the classroom where they were being interviewed. They were twins, impossible for a stranger to tell them apart, cheerful, round-faced and with complexions like the shell of a hazelnut.

They said they had put Roger Peters ashore on the quay at one o'clock in the morning. They had not seen anybody waiting for him but it had been raining hard and they had other things to think about. The one who admitted to being Billy said that he had taken Roger with him the previous afternoon when he had gone to Morvyl to do a repair job on Sam Tripp's wind-pump.

'We left about half past two and got back round seven.'

'Was Peters with you the whole time?'

'No, he stayed with the boat, mostly.'

Wycliffe got him to point out on the map where Sam Tripp's place was and noted that it lay just across the sound from Quincey Cove.

'Apart from yourselves, did Roger have any friends on the islands?'

The brothers looked at each other. 'Most of us was on good terms with Roger.' Billy added, after a moment's thought, 'I'm not sure if I know what you're after, Mr Wycliffe, but if I do, you can forget it. Roger wouldn't harm anybody.'

His brother, Henry, nodded, 'Nobody.'

Wycliffe spent the next hour on routine work with Gill. They asked the Plymouth police for information about Roger's lodgings and about his contacts in Plymouth.

Sergeant Scales reported having found prints of two fingers on the stainless-steel sink in the kitchen at Salubrious Place and the prints matched those on the filing cabinet in Vince Peters' room.

The telephone rang. It was the duty-officer to say that Peters' lawyer had arrived and wanted to see the chief superintendent. Wycliffe had a professional dislike of lawyers but this one was by no means true to type. Wycliffe thought that he must have been a 'one-off'. Young, with straggling blond hair, he wore a hipped-up version of a shooting jacket, light-brown cords and suede shoes.

'Tim Wells. I got your message about poor old Vince. Any ideas?'

Wycliffe waved him to a chair. 'No, Mr Wells, have you?'

'Me? Not a clue! We handled Vince's business but he was always close about his private life. All the same, there are one or two things you ought to know. First, there's big money involved, so his will is important.'

Wycliffe looked at the candid blue eyes and wondered if there was hope of a new breed of lawyer. 'You are willing to tell me about it?'

'Why the hell not? That's why I'm here. The will

is simple enough, taken by itself. Two hundred thousand and the house to his dolly girl and the residue to his brother.'

'You said, "taken by itself" . . .'

Wells nodded. 'I did. Most wills can be changed, some of our clients in the pop world, especially the women, change their wills as often as their hair styles. It's good for trade, but confusing.'

'But this will?'

'Was different.' The lawyer got out his cigarette case, offered round and lit up. 'Vince couldn't change it – at least, not the provision for his brother, that was the subject of an agreement.'

'Agreement? But in an agreement there must surely be some sort of quid pro quo?'

'There is, but it's vague – "in consideration of services rendered to the performing group known as . . ." blah, blah, blah.'

'Will it stand up?'

'It doesn't have to, the will is good. If Vince had changed his will it might have been a different matter but we took counsel's opinion.'

'When was that?'

'When the group wound up.'

'What does the residue amount to?'

Wells pursed his lips. 'Royalties, the residue of his capital . . . say, an income of twenty or thirty thousand a year.'

Wycliffe whistled. 'That's a great deal of money.'

'It's not peanuts.' Wells blew a thin thread of smoke ceiling-wards. 'This brother – where is he?'

Wycliffe was cautious. 'I understand that he is in the islands and we expect to contact him today.'

'When you do . . . '

'Of course. I'm grateful to you for your co-operation, Mr Wells. About the agreement you spoke of – what were its terms?'

'That Roger should receive not less than a half-share in the net value of the estate and Vince was precluded from making any deed of gift without the consent of his brother.'

'Extraordinary!'

'You're telling me!' Wells stood up. 'I suppose I'd better look in on the place. Is Clarissa there?'

Wycliffe offered him transport and the lawyer accepted. 'I'm not really the outdoor type. However, if you want me during the next day or so, I'm staying at The Garrison.' And Mr Wells drifted out.

When he had gone, Gill uncoiled himself from his chair. 'Like the man said, twenty or thirty thousand a year is more than peanuts, it's motive for murder.'

Wycliffe was drumming out a tattoo with his fingers on the desk top. 'And Sylvie?'

'There are a few things we don't know yet.'

Wycliffe grinned. 'Like the man said, "You're telling me!"' He got out his pipe and lit it. 'I'm worried about that gun. There's no doubt in my mind that the killer didn't just ditch it. If he was going to do that there would have been no point in taking the ammunition.'

Gill, for once, was serious. Policemen usually are when the talk is of guns. 'It worries me too but if we're right it alters the whole character of the case. It means we're due for another killing.'

Wycliffe stood up and walked over to the window. Rain was streaming down the glass, distorting his view. 'Not necessarily, it could be that he's the sort who feels safer with a gun and that he won't use it unless it comes to a showdown.'

'I don't know that that makes me feel any better.'

'Nor me.'

'In any case, there isn't much we can do about it.'

Wycliffe stared down at the deserted quay. 'We must warn our chaps to be careful; that goes for you, too.'

Jimmy Gill lit a cheroot and flicked the match in the general direction of the ashtray. 'Jackie Martin's alibi doesn't look so good by daylight, does it?'

It was true. Inspector Golly had organized a careful check on the times various people had left Charlie Martin's house after the funeral and, so far as Jackie Martin was concerned, there was conflicting testimony. It was possible that he had left as early as three o'clock, in which case he was still in the running. 'I can't see that boy with a gun,' Wycliffe said, 'but funnier things have happened.'

'He's kinky,' Gill said, spilling ash down the front of his suit.

The telephone rang. 'Brenda Luke is here, sir. She says she wants to add something to the statement she made – something she has remembered.'

'Bring her in.'

She came in, looking self-possessed and good enough to eat. Wet-look mac and shoes in red with a waterproof hat to match, her hair glistening with rain drops. She smiled at Gill but addressed herself to Wycliffe.

'Since I made my statement I remembered something. I can't really understand why I didn't think of it before.'

Wycliffe drew up a chair for her.

'I can't stay long. There's nothing doing in the ticket office this morning and I want to get back to Clarissa.

'It's just that your detective asked me if I'd seen anybody when I was on my way to the house yesterday afternoon. I said I hadn't but that wasn't true . . .'

'Well?'

'I saw Nick Marsden. You get so used to him hanging about, you don't take any notice.'

'Where, exactly, did you see him?'

'As I was crossing the bridge I saw him further down the valley. I suppose he was on his way home.'

'How far away?'

'It's difficult to say, I suppose a couple of hundred yards.'

'But you didn't see him while you were walking down the track from the moor?'

She shook her head. 'No, I didn't, that's what worries me.'

'Could he have come from the house?'

'If he'd come from the courtyard I would have seen him but he could have come from the back of the house, through the meadow.'

It might mean anything or nothing. There was no accounting for the movements of a man like Marsden.

She frowned. 'I'm a bit worried, I don't want to get him into trouble, but he was there . . .'

'I quite understand. Did he seem to be in a hurry?'

A pause. 'No, just like usual. He always looks as though he's going to fall over his feet the next step he takes.'

Wycliffe thanked her and arranged for her statement to be amended. When she had gone, Gill said, 'Marsden and Roger Peters were drinking buddies, don't you think we ought to bring Marsden in?'

Wycliffe shrugged. 'Maybe you're right.'

Gill sent Jordan to find him. The search did not take long. Marsden was propping up the bar of the Seymour. Despite the rain he had walked in with no more protection than his seaman's jersey. The public was unusually crowded because of the rain. None of the boats had gone out and most of the boatmen were there. The room was full of noise and smoke and the smell of wet wool. Charlie Martin was playing cribbage with the harbour master, the dominoes were out and others were playing whist.

Jordan had to push his way through to the bar. Charlie Martin followed him with his eyes. Marsden was drinking with Jack Bishop. The landlord was in the other bar for the visitors had nothing to do either. It was his daughter who greeted Jordan. 'The usual, Mr Jordan?'

'No, thanks, Clara, I wanted a word with Nick.'

Marsden was, as usual, not drunk but he had had quite a few. His skin, like his lips, was moist, he seemed to sweat beer and one had the impression that it might be squeezed out of him as from a sponge.

'You want me, Mr Jordan?'

He followed Jordan out, like a dog, and asked no questions until they reached the quay.

'Mr Gill will tell you what you need to know.'

In build and features there were resemblances between Marsden and Jimmy Gill. The huge frame, the rubbery features, thick lips and spiky hair, but the Chief Inspector was twenty-five years younger and in better shape.

Gill made him sit on a small, folding chair and sat himself on another, not two feet away. 'You know the score, Marsden, I'm not going to beat about the bush with you. Do you smoke?'

'Cigarettes.'

'You'll have to make do with one of these,' and he thrust one of his cheroots under the man's nose.

Marsden accepted the cheroot and lit it from Jimmy's lighter.

'I've just been speaking on the telephone to Peters' dolly-bird.'

'You mean, Miss Clarissa, I expect, Mr Gill.'

Gill gave him a dirty look and let it go. 'She told me that when they first went there, you used to do odd jobs about the place.'

Marsden was wary. 'I used to help out, neighbourly like.'

'Neighbourly, my arse! You used to make a few bob for yourself doing odd jobs and take the chance to nick what you could until Peters found you out.'

Marsden's protest was half-hearted.

'I don't care if you nicked the whole bloody outfit.' Gill thrust his stubbly chin forward and came a bit closer. 'I gather that one of the jobs you helped with was bringing a certain chest of drawers from one of the rooms upstairs down into the hall . . .'

'It's a long time ago . . .'

'Shut up! I'm not asking you, I'm telling you. In carrying the drawers down, you saw that there was a gun in one of them . . .'

'I never nicked no gun!'

'I didn't say that you nicked it, I said that you saw it.'

'I don't remember a gun.'

'You don't have to.'

Ash dropped down Marsden's cheroot on to the floor and Gill snapped, 'Don't make a bloody mess or you'll have to clear it up!' He allowed a small pause during which he pretended to consult some papers he held in his hand. Keep 'em guessing! 'Yesterday, a few minutes after Peters is known to have been shot, you were seen leaving the house. Everybody knows you hated his guts – and why. So!' Gill sat back with a dramatic gesture. 'What have we got?'

Marsden was gathering his wits and beginning to formulate some sort of reply but Gill interrupted. 'Don't say anything, you'd be wiser not to. We've got you, with motive, means and opportunity. Better men than you have found themselves in the topping shed for less, Marsden.'

The thick, moist lips hung loosely and Marsden looked at his interrogator with frightened eyes. 'You don't think . . .'

'Where's Roger Peters?'

It took a moment for Marsden to reorientate his thoughts. 'Roger?'

'Yes, where is he? He stood to gain a fortune by his brother's death. What was it? A deal between the two of you? What are you supposed to get out of it?'

Marsden shook his head in consternation. 'I don't

know where he is, Mr Gill, straight up, I don't. As for any deal . . .'

Gill's voice was venomous. 'If you're covering up for him, Marsden, you're a bigger bloody fool . . .'

'Christ! I can't afford to cover up for anybody in the spot I'm in! What is it you want me to do, Mr Gill?' He was sweating profusely and the beery smell, mixed with the odour of sodden wool, filled the room.

'I want your version of exactly what happened yesterday afternoon.'

It came fast enough. According to Marsden he had been on his way home. He'd left the Seymour at about two o'clock and by the time he reached Peters' place he was finding the heat a bit too much for him so he decided to have a kip in the bracken.

'Which side of the stream? This side or the house side?'

'This side, just below the bridge.'

'How long did you sleep?'

Marsden contorted his features into a semblance of contrition. 'I'd tell you if I knew, Mr Gill, but I ain't all that good on time, especially when I've had one or two.'

'All right. Then you woke up – what happened?'

'Something woke me. I thought it was a shot and there was what sounded like breaking glass. I said to meself it must be one of the boys trying to put the wind up Peters. Somebody putting a few shotgun pellets through one of his windows, I thought.'

'What did you do?'

Marsden wiped his forehead with a filthy rag. 'I sat up and took a gander but I couldn't see nobody so I went over. There was nobody in the yard and I couldn't see any broken window so I went round the back – into that bit of meadow . . .'

'Well?'

Marsden was getting increasingly agitated. 'I said I'd tell you the truth, Mr Gill . . .'

'You'd better!'

'Well, I soon spotted there was a broken window in the upstairs . . .'

'And?'

Marsden looked at the chief inspector as though trying to guess how far he was tying a noose round his own neck, then he decided to take the risk. 'I saw Peters slumped across the table – or desk, whatever it is by the window in that upstairs room.'

'But you didn't report what you had seen, you didn't even tell the officer who questioned you in the house-to-house.'

Marsden seemed to be appealing for reason. 'Well, I ask you, Mr Gill, I didn't want to find meself at the dirty end, did I?'

'Well, you're there now!' Gill snapped. 'I'm holding you for further questioning.' He lit another cheroot and gave it to Marsden.

'After that, I suppose, you went home?'

'I went home, Mr Gill. Yes, I did.'

'Did you meet anybody?'

Marsden choked on the smoke and had a lengthy fit of coughing. When he had recovered he said, 'No, I didn't meet anybody.'

'And are you quite sure you've no idea what time it was?'

The concentration was painful. 'I just thought of

something. Not long after I came out of the meadow I heard the siren of the old *Islander*.'

'What time would that be?'

Marsden scratched his head. 'When she's doing these day trips she'll cast off at half past four and she always gives a blast five minutes before to hurry 'em up.'

'Would that be ten minutes or longer after you heard the shot?'

'After I woke up? More like a quarter of an hour I should think but I never was much good on time.'

'And you saw nobody until you got home?'

'No, Mr Gill, I'd swear to that.'

'Nobody on the beach?'

He shook his head. 'No, but come to think, the Rowses' boat was drawn up on the shingle but there was nobody there.'

'Did you see anybody return to the boat later?'

'No, sir. I was all shook up and I went to bed. When I come down an hour or so later she were gone and I never thought any more about it.'

'Why should Peters' death shake you up?'

Marsden looked surprised. 'Why, it's obvious! As you said yourself, everybody knew I'd no good blood for Peters and there I was, on the spot, when he got it.'

'I'm very glad you appreciate your position,' Gill said. 'By the way, was what you told Mr Wycliffe true?'

'Gospel truth, Mr Gill! I'd swear it on my mother's head.'

Gill sniffed. 'Don't you ever wash?'

Marsden grinned. 'I must admit I'm not over fond of water, Mr Gill.'

Wycliffe was uneasy. He was sure that Peters' death must be linked with Sylvie's, yet the evidence, so far, seemed to point the other way. Roger Peters had a strong motive for killing his brother but what possible reason could he have had for murdering Sylvie? None of the mass of reports so painstakingly prepared gave any hint of a connection between them. The fact that Vince Peters had been murdered did not, of course, clear him of possible guilt for Sylvie's death, but it was inconceivable that the motives for the two crimes were unconnected. The obvious link between the killings was Jackie Martin, yet Roger Peters seemed to be doing his best to look like a guilty man. In any case, was it likely that Jackie Martin had shot Peters?

Jackie Martin. The boy intrigued him. Wycliffe was no psychologist but it would have been difficult not to see him as a textbook case. He had made a belated attempt to break out of the magic circle of possessive motherhood and failed . . . Given the talent, he might have found release for his pent-up frustrations in creative work, he might have grown into a Stendahl or a Lawrence. His books and his studious habits seemed to hint that he was dimly aware of the possibility of escape along that road. Given common-or-garden guts he might have persevered and stretched the silver cord until it snapped. In the event, it looked as though his frustration had exploded in a fit of juvenile rage in which he had knocked Humpty Dumpty for six.

And his mother. Some people seemed dogged by misfortune, ground down by circumstance. They are scarcely figures of tragedy for in tragedy there is an element of dignity. The Nellie Martins of this world live out their lives in drab misery, struggling against the odds, intensely jealous, possessive, bitterly resentful and worshipping the little grey god of respectability.

He was intrigued and repelled by the strange menage at the Tower House, and he sensed that only in their relationships would he find the explanations he sought.

It was still raining though less heavily. On the quay, a few visitors in raincoats and carrying umbrellas found the rain preferable to the anonymous drawing-rooms of their boarding houses. Although it was midday the lights were on in the saloon bar of the Seymour as he passed and they seemed to be doing good business.

Jackie, in his shirt sleeves, was seated at the table with a plate of stew in front of him and an open book beside his plate. The old man, in his chair beside the cooking range, was feeding himself with a spoon from a bowl supported on a board which rested across the arms of his chair. It seemed a miracle that his frail, trembling hand should ever guide the spoon to his mouth, but he managed.

Nellie Martin stood by the stove, one hand resting on the brass rod which ran just below the mantel-shelf. It was her customary place at mealtimes. Supervising. Waiting to offer somewhat belligerent service to her son and her husband. She would eat a mouthful herself between clearing away and washing up.

The windows were tight-shut. Water streamed down the panes behind the lace blinds and the atmosphere in the room was hot and humid.

Jackie never lifted his eyes from his book but neither did he turn the page.

When Wycliffe knocked on the front door, his mother went to one of the windows and lifted the blind aside then she turned to her son and nodded.

'I'll go upstairs,' Jackie said, getting up.

'No!'

She went to the door. 'What is it now?' Weary and aggressive at the same time.

'I want to talk to your son, Mrs Martin.'

'We're having our meal.'

Without waiting to be invited he took off the oilskin coat he was wearing and hung it on one of the pegs in the hall where it dripped on to the red-tiled floor. He came into the kitchen and sat on a chair by the windows. Jackie acknowledged him with a glance then looked down at his book. His mother went over to her place by the stove. Nobody spoke. The old man looked at Wycliffe from time to time with eyes which had long since ceased to question. An alarm clock ticked loudly on the mantelshelf and the stove crackled. The old man let his spoon fall into the fender. His wife picked it up and gave it to him. For the second time she asked, 'What is it now?'

She might well ask, he hardly knew himself.

'Don't you go to the Peters place any more, Mrs Martin?'

'Is there any reason why I shouldn't?'

Wycliffe shrugged.

'I don't go there until the afternoon on Thursdays.'

Jackie was scarcely touching his food and his eyes never left his book.

'When were you last at the house, Mr Martin?'

'Me?' Jackie looked up, startled.

'He was there on Tuesday night.' Tight-lipped.

'Not yesterday?'

'Yesterday he went to the funeral.'

'And afterwards?'

'He went to his uncle's, most of the mourners did.'

'What time did you leave your uncle's, Mr Martin?'

This time he was allowed to answer for himself. 'I can't say exactly but it must have been about four.'

'He came in here at twenty past four. I noticed because I was cooking a few buns and that was when they were due to come out.'

'Did you know that Peters had a gun?'

'No, I didn't, I swear!'

It was remarkable. Through all this the old man went on with his meal. Now his plate was empty and he started to wave his spoon about in an agitated fashion. His wife took the plate and put in its place a bowl containing some sort of milk pudding. The ritual of feeding continued.

'Why did you go to see Peters on Tuesday night?'

'I often go there.'

'I know, you told me. But Sylvie was murdered on Saturday night. On Tuesday when I talked to you, you were deeply distressed . . .'

'That's natural enough!' Tartly, from his mother.

'Quite natural. What surprises me is to hear that you were paying a social call the same evening.'

'I had to talk to Peters.'

'About Sylvie?'

Jackie stared down at his plate with unfocused eyes.

His mother intervened. 'He couldn't just do nothing!'

'Did you accuse Peters?'

'No, when I got there he and Clarissa were playing cards and I couldn't see him alone.'

'So what did you do?'

His reply was all but inaudible. 'I played cards with them.'

Wycliffe had heard that Jackie's clothes, which had been sent to forensic, had been collected when his mother was out. He doubted if Jackie had told his mother.

'Well, that's all for the moment. If all goes well, we shall be returning your clothes in a day or two.'

'What clothes?'

Jackie was silent.

'What clothes?' She moved closer to the table.

'My fawn trousers and sports jacket.'

'You said you'd sent them to the cleaners.'

'I didn't want to worry you, mother.'

She turned to Wycliffe. 'Why did you take his clothes?'

'For routine examination. Your son's are not the only clothes which are being examined.'

She looked from Wycliffe to Jackie and back again, trying to assess this new threat. Wycliffe felt more than a twinge of compassion but he had a job to do.

After lunch the rain eased, then stopped. Wycliffe and Gill were driven in the Land-Rover to Salubrious Place. The downs were like a green sponge and brown water oozed out of the soil and trickled across the track collecting in the ruts and potholes. In the valley the bridge was barely clear of the stream which had turned into a brown torrent.

Wycliffe, who hated keeping people waiting about, sent the Land-Rover back. 'I'll call if I need you.' He was keeping an appointment with Clarissa but Gill was on his way to Quincey Cove. The only way was to walk down the valley – unless you had a boat.

Clarissa was cordial, she seemed genuinely glad to see him. She took him into the large, opulent sitting-room which had one wall entirely of glass and made Wycliffe feel like a goldfish. Water was still trickling down the glass and the meadow appeared as kaleidoscopic patterns of greens. The cats prowled restlessly, jumping up on to the furniture and down again. 'They are not happy indoors but they do not like getting their paws wet.'

She wore a black jumper and skirt with a gold chain round her neck and a small cross at her breast. She was almost certainly a Catholic which must have added to her problems. She was pale and her beautiful eyes were puffed with much crying. But her manner now was perfectly controlled. She thanked Wycliffe for being considerate. 'Brenda is staying with me – she is gone to the farm at the moment, but she has been much help.' Her precise enunciation and the vagaries of her syntax made her, somehow, more pathetic, more appealing.

'There are a few questions.'

'Of course!' She perched herself on the edge of one of the huge, black armchairs and waited like an obedient schoolgirl.

Wycliffe was feeling the bowl of his pipe in his pocket. When he could not smoke it was his consolation.

'Light your pipe, Mr Wycliffe, I am sure you will feel much at home.'

He accepted gratefully. 'I believe you had a visit from Mr Wells, this morning?'

She nodded. 'Vince's lawyer, yes, he was here.'

'I expect he told you about the will?'

'Yes.' Her manner was casual as though it was a matter of no importance. 'But I already knew, Vince told me that was what he would do.' She blinked rapidly and dabbed her eyes with her handkerchief. 'You will excuse me, please.'

'You also knew of the provision for Roger?'

She shook her head. 'No, I did not know that but I am not surprised. Vince was very good to his brother, always giving him money.'

Wycliffe was staring at an aggressive, abstract painting in flaring reds. 'Have you ever thought that Roger might have had some hold over his brother?'

She looked at him quickly. 'Yes, I have thought that sometimes. Is it true?'

It was Wycliffe's turn to shake his head. 'I don't know.' But he was beginning to have the germ of an idea. The possible significance of what he had seen in Peters' room dawned on him. He smoked his pipe in silence for a while.

Clarissa became uneasy as the silence lengthened.

Outside, although it was no longer raining, the sky was overcast and, despite the huge windows and the fact that it was the middle of a summer afternoon, the room was only dimly lit. Clarissa shivered, got up and went over to the switches by the door. The two ceiling lights sprang to life. 'It is like winter,' she said, nervously.

Wycliffe agreed that it was but his thoughts had moved on. 'When did you decide to go shopping on the mainland?'

She was surprised by the question. 'I do not know. I go about once a month and it is not a thing to plan very much . . .'

'Except that it has to be on Nellie's day off.'

For an instant her face lit up with a smile. 'That is right. I expect Brenda told you, Vince did not like Nellie.'

'Why not?'

Her forehead wrinkled in a deep frown. 'She disapproved of him. She is – how do you say – narrow-minded. Is that right? Vince say she is like his mother was and it makes him feel uncomfortable.' She smiled again. 'Vince was silly about such things, he took too much notice. All the same he would provoke her by pretending to be very bad when he is not.'

'Why didn't he sack her?'

She shook her head. 'I cannot explain, he was like that. Some things he feel he must put up with. Also she is a very good worker and she had a very hard life.'

Wycliffe had turned the interrogation into a conversation and that was what he usually aimed to do.

'I should have thought that with Jackie single, earning quite good money as a schoolteacher, she would not have needed to go out to work.'

Clarissa shrugged. 'She is very independent and will not accept what she calls charity from her son. Also, Jackie is an only child and a little selfish so I do not think he will try very hard to persuade her.'

Wycliffe nodded. He was gradually getting to know these people so that what they did and said no longer surprised him. It was like doing a complicated jigsaw puzzle: at first there is very little logic in the procedure, then the pattern begins to emerge and finally a stage is reached when it is possible to predict what will eventually fill the blank spaces. He had not reached that stage yet but he was making progress.

'Is it possible that Vince had an appointment yesterday and wanted the house to himself?'

She took him up quickly. 'You mean a woman? If so, you do not understand. Vince did not hide such things from me, he did not have to. His life as a great pop star . . .' She spread her hands in an expressive gesture. 'Of course he had many women, it was part of the life – you understand?'

'And now – recently?'

Her face clouded. 'You know that Vince was very sick?'

Wycliffe nodded.

'It affected his heart and it was no longer wise . . .' Another telling gesture. 'He was advised by the doctor . . . All the same, there is lung cancer and I do not see the tobacco shops close their doors.' Again she was very near to tears.

Wycliffe was gentle. 'You do not have to tell me.'

'But I must! You will find out who it is that killed him. There were not many affairs of late but the silly girls . . . some of them.'

'Sylvie?'

'Especially Sylvie. For her I felt sorry, I think she loved him, for the others, he was a symbol – you understand?'

'You know that Sylvie was going to have a child?'

'Yes, I know. Vince told me. Poor girl!' She was silent for a time. 'How foolish! If only she had known. We wondered if she had killed herself because . . .'

'She was murdered.'

'I know that now.' She raised her eyes to his. 'You cannot think that Vince . . . ?'

'Do you?'

'Oh, no! It is not possible. If you knew him you would not think so. Vince could be cruel, but in words or by his silence . . . I have never known him do anything violent – never! It was not in his nature.'

Another long silence while Wycliffe smoked. The windows were clearer and brighter, the clouds must be thinning.

'When I suggested that he might have had an appointment, I was not thinking of a woman.'

She frowned. 'I see. It is possible but I do not think so. I cannot think of anything Vince would try to hide from me. Some things he did not tell me but he would not try to stop me knowing.'

It was strange to hear her speak of Peters as she saw him through the eyes of love. His self-centred indifference became almost a virtue.

'He was very lucky to meet you when he did.'

She accepted his statement as an English girl would not, without any false modesty. 'Yes, it was at the right time – the psychological moment, as you say. Already there were signs of his illness, he would fumble the fingering of his guitar and sometimes he would have the double vision. It was in Paris that he realized he could not go on.' She looked at him with grave, sad eyes. 'You can imagine the effect on him, it was lucky I was there.'

'I understand that Roger was his manager?'

'That was what he was called but I did not see him do much.'

'From what I have heard, I wouldn't have thought him a very good business man.'

She smiled. 'You are right! Roger was like a child in business and Vince had to do all the real work.' She shifted a little irritably in her chair. 'That is why I become a little angry when he is here all the time asking for money . . .'

They talked for a while longer but Wycliffe learned nothing new. When he stepped into the courtyard there were patches of hazy blue in the sky, the clouds were breaking up. He decided to walk back.

Chapter Eight

Now that the rain had stopped the level of the stream fell rapidly which was as well for in places the path was broken away and there were gravelly, rocky stretches which had been submerged by the stream in flood. As Gill left Salubrious Place behind him the valley became more desolate and the sides steeper, with outcrops of granite sparsely covered with grey lichens. Fescue grass and clumps of sea-pinks covered the valley floor which was strewn with great grey boulders.

The clouds had melted away on the horizon but overhead they were still heavy and lowering. Despite this it was very warm. He began to sweat and took off his jacket. Nowhere could he see anything recognizable as the handiwork of man and landscapes without figures were, for him, a dead waste of space. Not for him, the wind on the heath, brother, nor the lonely sea and the sky. A few blocks of flats within easy reach of the local and a good supermarket was the landscape of his choice. But the scenery on the island consisted of landscapes in miniature and soon the valley became broader and shallower once more, the stream fanned out over gravel and finally lost itself in a broad beach of sharp, white sand. He was at Quincey Cove.

On his right and near at hand, a row of three stark little cottages stared blankly out to sea. The area in front of them was littered with junk of every description, some of it housed in decayed, make-shift sheds, most of it in jumbled heaps. To his left, across a narrow stretch of calm water, the southern tip of Morvyl was just in view. A low, rocky promontory, a tiny, white cove with a boat drawn up on the sand and, inland, three or four whitewashed buildings in a group and a slender, iron-framed tower with a windmill on the top. Presumably, Sam Tripp's wind pump.

Three children were playing on the rough ground between the mounds of junk and Gill went over to them. The eldest, a girl of seven or eight, immediately scurried into the nearest house like a frightened rabbit, the other two, boys of five or six, continued inexplicable labours on a go-kart made from a fish-box and pram wheels. Gill waited by the open door through which the little girl had disappeared. A dirty, green-painted screen prevented him from seeing into the room but he could hear low voices. Then an older girl, who looked eighteen but was probably younger, came round the screen. She was plump and stocky, a V-necked flowery dress, in need of washing, showed most of her bosom which had never known Playtex control. She was black-eyed with a mop of dark hair which looked as though she combed it with her fingers. She looked at him with a mixture of aggression and apprehension. She had an earthy, animal vitality which was not lost on Gill.

'Police.'

'What we supposed to 've done now?'

'Nothing. It's what other people have done.'

'Not our business!'

'Who is it, Moira?' A cracked old voice.

'I'll tell you in a minute – be quiet!' She added, under her breath, 'Silly ol' cow!'

'Your grandmother?'

'She's me great-great-grandmother – ninety-eight she is.'

'You are Moira Marsden?'

'If it's any concern of yours.' But her aggression had gone with her apprehension and she was merely being flirtatious.

Gill smiled his great rubbery smile, a real baby-frightener, but it went down well with the girls.

'I suppose you see most of what goes on round here?'

She looked at the empty beach and the empty sea. 'Job not to.'

'Do you know Roger Peters?'

'Sort of.'

'Ever see him about here?'

'Now and then.'

'When was the last time?'

She sniffed. 'Yesterday it must 've bin. He come across from Morvyl in the Rowses' boat.'

'By himself?'

She nodded. 'He pulled the boat up on the shingle an' stuck the kedge in the sand.' She grinned. 'If he'd been gone much longer he'd had to swim for it. Tide come up the beach pretty fast.'

'What time was this?'

She looked vague. 'Round teatime when he come back, I reckon.'

'When's that?'

'Between five an' six.'

'How long was he gone?'

She was getting tired of his sustained interest in someone else. There were more important things. 'How do I know? What do it matter, anyway?'

'How long?'

'Might 've bin an hour or an hour an' a half. I tell you I didn't take that much notice.'

'But you know he came from Morvyl?'

'I saw him, didn't I? He put Billy Rowse ashore on the point, he hung about there for a bit, then he come over here, like I said. What you on about?'

'Did your father come home while Roger Peters was away up the valley?'

'He'd 've had a job, he bin dead five year an' more. Fell overboard when he was drunk.'

'I'm sorry.'

'I ain't, he was a bastard.'

'I was talking about Nick Marsden.'

'Oh, he's me grandfather. Yeh, he did come home.'

'Did he mention having seen either of the Peters brothers?'

'He never mentioned nothing, he was drunk like usual an' he went to bed.'

Gill turned on the charm. 'Thanks, Moira.'

She looked at him big-eyed. 'I could fancy you.'

'I'll be around.'

He left her, standing in the doorway, looking after him.

On his way back from Salubrious Place Wycliffe met the widow woman from the café, doing her shopping along the quay. She smiled at him, ruefully, but he thought he saw a glint of mischief in her eye. He had a soft spot for her and wondered why she had stayed unmarried. Perhaps she had found a way to get the best of both worlds but he doubted it. Not with Roger Peters.

He climbed the steep slope to the school, thinking. In the operations room he stopped to speak to Jordan who was duty-officer. 'Any news of Peters?'

'Nothing, sir. It's a bit of a puzzle really, we've got half our strength on it but so far we've drawn a blank. To be frank, I don't think any islander would risk a harbouring charge for Roger Peters. It's one thing to have a drink with a man or go fishing but it's quite another to fall foul of the police in a murder case.' Jordan scratched his ear. 'It's my belief that he must be sleeping rough somewhere. There's plenty of places where a man could lie up for days if he had a bit of food with him. But it's only a matter of time . . .'

'What about the widow woman?'

'What about her?'

'Wouldn't she risk a harbouring charge?'

Jordan looked puzzled. 'She might, but he can't be there. We've had the place watched since you left last night.'

'Not exactly.' Wycliffe lowered his voice so that a young detective working near by could not hear what he said. 'Send a couple of chaps along there to bring him in.'

'You mean . . . ?'

'I mean I've been taken for a sucker again. While I was walking from the café to your place last night,

Peters nipped in and by the time our man went on obo that precious couple were tucked up in bed.' He chuckled. 'And she had the cheek to offer me her umbrella!'

In his office he found a new crop of typescript which had sprouted in his tray. Among the rest, a memorandum from the Plymouth CID which they had telephoned in reply to his enquiry about Roger Peters. Obviously it had been compiled by some Jack with a nice feeling for atmosphere, which pleased Wycliffe.

'Subject occupies a rented room at 14, Frobisher Place. Frobisher Place comprises three large houses once occupied by high-ranking naval personnel, now cheap lodging houses . . .' (A note of satisfaction there, surely?) 'According to his landlady, Peters' tenancy began six months ago. He is away from home a great deal and has told her that he is a travelling salesman. To her knowledge, he has no visitors but he receives a certain amount of mail, mainly business letters to judge from the envelopes. She says that he is "a nice man, keeps himself to himself and pays his rent regular". Our officer had the impression that there may be a more intimate relationship between Peters and his landlady.' Peters must have a considerable talent for obtaining free digs.

'The landlady had a key to his room and allowed our man to inspect it. The room was shabby and not too clean. A minimum of battered furniture which went with the room was supplemented by items belonging to Peters. These included a good upright piano, a studio couch, a record player with a stack of records, a tape recorder and two guitars. In the clothes cupboard there were two good suits and three or four silk shirts along with other shirts and underclothes bought at a department store. There were few papers in the room but a box-file contained several letters about electrical goods for which he appears to have an agency.

'Further inquiries established that he frequents the Barbican area of the city and that he is on friendly terms with several of the boatmen. He is a customer at the betting-shop in that area and is believed to be in debt there . . .'

While he was going through the report Gill came in and they brought each other up to date.

'You really think he's at the café?'

'We shall soon know.' Wycliffe got up and went over to the window. The sun was shining now from a clear, rain-washed sky but it had come too late for the boats were still riding at their moorings. No doubt there would be evening trips. The quay was unusually crowded for the time of day with visitors parading up and down. The *Islander* was at her berth embarking day-trippers for the return crossing but there were very few because of the morning's rain.

The case against Roger Peters was beginning to take shape. He was forced to consider, very seriously, the possibility that Sylvie's death and the shooting of Vince Peters were two unconnected crimes. According to Nellie Martin, Vince had asked his brother to come to the house between half past three and four on the day of his death. Now, Gill had firm evidence that Roger had kept the appointment, and, more significantly, Marsden claimed to have heard a shot at about ten minutes past four. As Marsden did not meet Roger on his way to the cove there were reasonable grounds for believing that Roger must have been in the house when the shot was fired. It was by no means a cast-iron case but the circumstantial evidence was strong and men had been convicted on no more.

Gill was seated by his desk, browsing through reports. 'You think he did it?'

'He had motive, means and opportunity.'

'But do you think he did it?'

Wycliffe did not answer directly. He moved away from the window. 'They've found him, he's on his way up.'

The siren of the *Islander* blared, warning all laggards.

Five minutes later Peters was brought in. He looked pale under his tan, and worried. He might have spent part of the night in the widow's bed but it was obvious that he had not slept. Wycliffe waved him to a chair. 'Would you object to having your fingerprints taken, Mr Peters?'

'Would it make any difference if I did?'

Gill leered. 'It might – at this stage.'

Peters shrugged and Wycliffe picked up the telephone. 'Is Sergeant Scales in? Ask him to come here with his gear.'

Scales came in with his case, the prints were taken and Peters was given cleaning tissues to remove the ink from his fingers. When Scales had finished he glanced at Wycliffe and Wycliffe gave a small sign. Scales left with his case. The operation had taken less than five minutes. Gill shifted his chair so that he was on Wycliffe's side of the desk.

'Why did you hide away?'

He looked at Wycliffe through tired, blue eyes. 'How can you say I was hiding? You know I live there when I'm in the islands.'

Wycliffe was patient. 'You knew the police wanted to interview you and you deliberately evaded them.'

'I heard that Vince was dead – that he had been murdered, and I was scared.'

'Why?'

'Wendy said you seemed all set to latch it on me and I was the obvious one anyway.'

'Because of the will?'

Peters said nothing.

'You know about your brother's will?'

A momentary hesitation. 'Yes.'

'You couldn't have expected to stay out of circulation for long.'

Peters stared at the floor. 'No, but I thought it might be long enough for you to find out who did it.'

'So you deny shooting your brother?'

'Of course I deny it! I didn't do it.' He was fingering his moustache with nervous fingers.

'Did you know that your brother possessed a gun?'

Peters, staring down at the parquet flooring, was mumbling his answers so that they were scarcely audible. 'I knew that he bought one, it was while we were in the States in '68.'

'Did he feel threatened?'

'What?' Peters looked up. It was as though he were preoccupied, trying to make up his mind about something and Wycliffe's questions intruded on his thoughts. 'No, it wasn't that he felt threatened, he just bought it for kicks.'

'Do you know where he kept it?'

'I didn't know that he still had it.'

There was little family resemblance. Roger was of a stockier build than his brother and his hair was fair with only a trace of auburn. Although he had sideboards and a Gerald Nabarro moustache he had no beard to hide his weak chin.

'When did you last visit your brother?'

'Thursday, I think it was – yes, last Thursday, a week ago today.'

'That was when you quarrelled?'

Peters looked up sharply. 'We had an argument.'

'About money?'

He nodded. 'I suppose Clarissa told you.'

'Yesterday, Wednesday, where were you?'

'When?'

Wycliffe made an irritable movement. 'Any time – all day.'

There was a small silence while he thought over his answer, either to recollect or invent. 'I got up late and did a few chores for Wendy to keep the peace, then I went along to the Seymour for a jar.'

'Then?'

'Well, when I was coming out I met Billy Rowse and he said he had to go over to Morvyl in the afternoon to do a job on Sam Tripp's water pump so I said I would tag along.'

'Time?'

'I had my lunch first and we got to Morvyl about half-two.'

'And you left – when?'

'Just after six.'

'Were you with Rowse the whole time?'

'No, we went ashore at Penhallick Cove and I stayed with the boat. The cove is close to Sam's place.'

'You stayed with the boat for more than three hours?'

'I must have done.'

'Did you see anyone during that time?'

Peters frowned. 'I don't think so, it's a quiet spot.'

Wycliffe grunted. 'It must be.' The telephone rang and Wycliffe answered it. 'Wycliffe.'

It was Sergeant Scales. 'I'll speak quietly, sir. His prints match those we found on the cabinet in Peters' room and on the sink in the kitchen.'

'No possible doubt?'

'No, sir.'

Wycliffe dropped the receiver and turned to Peters. He looked at him in silence for a while. Peters met his eye and seemed, suddenly, to become aware that a new element had entered into the interrogation.

'I don't want to trap you into further lies, Mr Peters, so I will caution you, then I will tell you exactly what we know about your movements on the afternoon your brother was shot.'

Peters listened to the caution but said nothing.

'We know that you had an appointment with your brother yesterday afternoon. We also know that you used the Rowses' boat to cross the sound from Morvyl to Quincey Cove. At approximately ten minutes past four Nick Marsden heard a shot fired in your brother's house, he saw the broken window and he also saw your brother slumped over his desk. He then walked down the valley to his cottage at Quincey Cove; he did not meet you but when he got to the cove the Rowses' boat was drawn up on the beach.'

Peters sat staring at the floor, his hands clasped tightly round his knees, saying nothing.

'There is one other piece of evidence. Your fingerprints – fresh prints – were found on the filing cabinet in your brother's room and on the sink in the kitchen.'

For a time Peters gave no sign, then he relaxed and sat back in his chair staring straight at Wycliffe. 'I knew it would be like this!'

'You admit that you shot your brother?' From Gill.

He shook his head listlessly. 'No, but how can I prove that I didn't against all that?'

'You don't have to. All you have to do is to explain the facts as they affect you. Do you wish to make a statement?'

After a moment of hesitation Peters nodded.

'Before you do, are you willing to answer some further questions?'

'I suppose so.'

'Do you admit visiting your brother on the afternoon he died?'

'Yes, but he was dead when I got there.' Wycliffe said nothing and, after a while, Peters continued. 'Like you said, Vince phoned me and asked me to come to see him. He didn't say what it was about but I knew that it was about money. When I heard that Billy Rowse was going to Sam's place on Morvyl

I thought it would be easier to slip across from there with the boat rather than walk all the way from the town.'

'You weren't bothered about being seen by the Marsdens?'

'No – why should I be? I didn't know I was going to find him shot, did I?' He seemed surprised and pleased to find this point in his favour.

'Were you in the house when the shot was fired?'

'No, I wasn't. I know it looks bad but the reason Nick Marsden didn't see me was because I saw him first, stumbling along beside the stream, more than half-pissed as usual. Nick can be a bloody nuisance when he's drunk – maudlin, so I dodged him. Actually I got to the house at half past four.'

'What happened when you got there?'

'Nothing happened. I went in by the back door and through into the hall. I called but nobody answered so I went up to his room where he spends most of his time . . . Of course, I found him.'

'What did you do?'

He shook his head. 'I was knocked sideways. Vince and I have been pretty close through the best part of our lives . . . .'

'Did you touch him?'

He nodded again. 'I wanted to be sure.'

'How do you account for your fingerprints on the cabinet?'

'I don't know but it's quite likely I rested against it – I had quite a job to stop myself from fainting.'

'What did you do then?'

He seemed to be in the grip of considerable emotion and there was an interval before he started to speak again. 'I went back downstairs, I don't know what I would have done but when I was in the hall I noticed that my right hand felt sticky . . . When I looked I saw that it had blood and stuff . . . I don't know how it got there, I must have touched . . .' He shuddered. 'I went into the kitchen to wash it off and while I was there the girl came in at the front door and called out.' He looked at Wycliffe. 'I have never been so frightened in my life.' His eyes had become wild at the recollection. 'I just went out of the back door and ran until I couldn't run any more.'

'Down the valley?'

'Down the valley to the boat.' He added, after a moment, choking over the words, 'It's no good, I can't explain it.'

In the silence they could hear noises from the quay, even the sound of voices. Gill took out his cheroots and offered one to Peters. Peters refused.

'Do you believe me?'

'You were your brother's business manager, is that right?' Gill asked the question while he was lighting his cheroot.

'Yes.'

Gill took his time. 'There was an agreement, wasn't there? Between you and your brother, an agreement in which he undertook to leave you the bulk of his estate.'

Peters nodded.

'What did he get out of it?'

Peters answered with what dignity he could muster. 'My services, I suppose.'

'As his business manager? You must be joking!'

Wycliffe was almost sorry for the man. He said,

quite casually, 'Your brother never wrote a song in his life, did he?'

This was a blow he had not expected and he reacted slowly. 'I don't know what you mean.'

'I think you do.'

Wycliffe and Gill watched him while he considered the new threat. At last he reached a decision and seemed to resign himself. His manner was more relaxed as though he had got rid of a burden.

'In the beginning it was a question of tactics I suppose. For years, while Vince was at school and I was working as an assistant in a music shop, I tried my hand at song-writing. I never came within a mile of success. Then, when Vince was at University, he started to make a name for himself as a singer, first it was no more than a student thing, then he started to enter for talent contests and after that the clubs got interested. His trouble was to find good, new songs and one day I suggested he should try one of mine . . . It was Kalamazoo Baby . . . Through a mistake, I suppose it was, everybody thought he had written it himself and we decided it would be best to leave it at that – to concentrate on building him up.' He stopped talking, reached in his pocket for a packet of cigarettes and lit one before going on.

'Vince and I got on well together. Even working like we did – for years – in the pop racket, I can't remember a single real row. When things started to go big I was nominally his manager but Gus Clayton and Vince did most of the business side between them. Everybody thought I was a passenger, a poor relation. Well, it didn't hurt me and it was all good for the Vince image. One day Vince said he thought we ought to have an agreement – in case anything happened to him. He told me that he'd made a will. It was more a joke than anything else but in the end we drew up a sort of agreement. I didn't take it seriously and things went on as before . . . Until Paris, two years ago.' He broke off. 'You know that Vince was very ill?'

Wycliffe nodded.

'When he realized that he wasn't going to get better he changed.'

'Not surprising, really.'

Peters was anxious to be clearly understood. 'No, I don't suppose it was, he had to give up singing, the kind of life he was leading would have killed him in three months, the doctors said . . . His complaint had affected his heart or he had a weak heart as well. You could have understood it if he was damn near suicidal, but he wasn't. He took it all very calmly, he bought this place down here and settled down, more or less. But he'd changed, his character had changed. I couldn't get near him any more. And he got mean. I don't want to sound greedy but he was rolling in it and I had a claim to a good slice of the royalties, at least, but he wouldn't see it. You would think I was asking for charity. All he would say was, "Don't be in such a hurry, you'll be all right when I'm gone." ' Peters stopped and seemed to want his point to sink in. 'Well, it wasn't good enough and I threatened to blow the gaff. I didn't want to. For one thing it would probably have had a bad effect on sales and, in any case, the last thing I really wanted was to hurt Vince. I don't think I would have done it when it came to the point.'

'What happened?'

'Vince said I was being unreasonable. He showed me letters which had passed between him and his lawyer about his will but he wouldn't give in . . .'

'This was the row you had a week before he died?'

Peters nodded. 'And I heard nothing more from him until he telephoned for me to come and see him.'

'You are willing to put all this into a statement?'

'Yes.'

Wycliffe signed to Gill and Gill took him out.

At the door he turned. 'You believe me, don't you?'

Wycliffe made a noncommittal gesture.

Did he believe Peters? He had to admit that he had been favourably impressed by his apparent frankness. But the frankness had followed an absurd attempt to hide and patent lies. He was weak, there was no question about that, but weakness is no testament to innocence. In Wycliffe's experience, violent crime was more often than not the work of weak, usually stupid people. And in some ways Peters was stupid, at any rate, limited.

But what about Sylvie? It always came back to the same question and he seemed as far as ever from getting an answer. He found himself saying aloud, 'There is not a shred of evidence to connect Roger Peters with Sylvie's death.'

There was no evidence to connect Peters with Sylvie's death but, all the same, he was still convinced that the second death had followed the first as part of the same criminal act.

'The press and TV people are here, they want to know if you are holding Peters.'

Since the morning the islanders had been intrigued, flattered and irritated by the antics of a TV reporter and camera team.

He made a statement, standing in front of the school, his fine, sandy hair blowing in the wind. On the 'News' that evening, they would be saying, 'Two men were at the Murder Headquarters of Detective Chief Superintendent Wycliffe today, helping with inquiries. Both made statements and later left. Chief Superintendent Wycliffe, Head of Area Crime Squad, spoke to our reporter:

'Are you satisfied with the progress of your inquiries, Mr Wycliffe?'

'I am not satisfied – no. I shall only be satisfied when an arrest has been made, but we are making progress.'

'Do you expect to make an arrest in the near future?'

'I hope that an arrest may be made shortly.'

'Would you care to comment on statements that Vince Peters' death could have been the result of an island vendetta against him?'

'I know of no vendetta.'

'Is it true that the islanders have resented your presence and that they have made your task more difficult?'

'No, it is not true. On the contrary, we have received a great deal of cooperation from the islanders.'

'Do you consider that the Vince Peters' shooting and the death of Sylvie Eva are connected?'

'I do not want to comment on that point at this stage.'

When the circus had gone his thoughts reverted to their original theme. If Roger Peters did not shoot his brother, who did? He had ideas on the subject but ideas are not proof. Back in his office he made notes on a memo pad, a thing he rarely did.

Nick Marsden heard the shot at 4.10.

Marsden hung about the house until 4.20.

Brenda Luke arrived at about 4.30 and went to the pottery.

Roger Peters arrived at the back of the house through the meadow also at about 4.30.

He regarded what he had written with distaste. It seemed most likely that the murderer had left the house between 4.20 and 4.30 but Roger Peters, coming up the valley, had seen only Marsden. Brenda Luke, coming from town, had also seen Marsden and no-one else.

Presumably the murderer had taken all possible steps not to be seen. All the same . . .

Wycliffe went to the Jordans for his evening meal. Fish pie followed by junket and cream. Jordan was on duty so Wycliffe ate his meal in the little kitchen with Mrs Jordan hovering round him.

After a while she said, 'I suppose you heard about the fuss on the quay this afternoon?'

'No.'

'The chap from the TV – he caught Jack Bishop coming out of the Seymour and started asking him questions about what the islanders thought of Peters. Was there a vendetta – that sort of carry on. Jack had had enough to drink and he was ready to talk, but just then, along comes Charlie Martin.'

'What happened?'

A short laugh. 'He stood in front of the camera and told them if they didn't move he would throw them and their camera in the harbour. I was out shopping. It made quite a stir.'

After his meal Wycliffe walked along the quay. Another warm, peaceful evening with a mackerel sky high over the sea. The tide was at full flood and the boats in the harbour were almost level with the quay. There was to be dancing later and the town band was already in position, warming up.

In the public bar of the Seymour, Charlie Martin was talking very seriously with Matthew Eva who looked old and drawn. Neither of them accorded him more than a bare acknowledgment. Wycliffe ordered a beer and took a seat near the counter. It was, presumably, like any other summer evening in the Seymour. Two hands of whist, a game of chequers and three or four men sitting round, sipping their beer and saying little. Yet Wycliffe was aware of an atmosphere of tension. Everyone in the bar seemed to be waiting, marking time. Rightly or wrongly, he felt that they were waiting for him. Waiting for him to point the accusing finger – and go! Get it over!

It was not long before Matthew finished his drink and left. Charlie Martin, who had his back to the bar, twisted round in his seat until he could see Wycliffe.

'Will you be so kind as to join me, Mr Wycliffe?'

Wycliffe took his drink to the old man's table. The eyes of everyone in the bar were on him.

Charlie Martin's huge, freckled hands rested on the table and his fingers beat out a gentle tattoo. 'Have you made up your mind, Mr Wycliffe?'

Wycliffe smoked his pipe in silence for a while. 'I have made up my mind but I still need evidence.'

The old man nodded as though it was the reply he had expected. 'We are not murderers, Mr Wycliffe, neither do we condone murder.'

'I am glad to hear it.'

'Peters alive was one thing, Peters dead – shot, is another.'

Wycliffe's bland expression did not change. When it came to Arab tea parties he could hold his own.

'One of your young men has questioned me twice about what happened after the girl's funeral; in particular he wanted to know when my nephew left the house after it was over. I told him that the boy was with me until four o'clock and that was the truth.'

'I have no doubt of it.'

The old man's blue eyes rested for a moment on Wycliffe's in shrewd appraisal. 'The boy was distressed – in a bad way. Once or twice while we were following the hearse and again during the committal, I thought that he would collapse.'

Wycliffe said nothing. Martin's ringed finger rapped on the tabletop. 'Let's have something a bit stronger than this cat's piss, Mr Wycliffe. Two brandies, if you please, Jonathan – large ones.'

The barman brought the drinks and the two men did not speak until they were about to sip the brandy. 'Your health!'

For once the old man was uncertain how to play his hand and Wycliffe would not help him. 'Mother love can be a terrible thing, Mr Wycliffe – a crippling thing. The boy is more to be pitied than blamed.'

He took out a large red handkerchief with white spots and patted his moustache. 'Love is only one side of the coin, Mr Wycliffe; hate is the other.'

The silence in the bar was impressive. Wycliffe had not heard a single word spoken by the other occupants of the bar since he had moved to Martin's table.

'In a small community like ours it is necessary that we stand together, there must be loyalty. But, as I said, we do not condone murder.'

Outside, on the quay, the band was playing and they were dancing.

'Jackie's father is my half-brother, he was the son of a second wife. I would have helped. A full-time nurse – day and night if necessary, or a nursing home. But Nellie was too proud, she made a virtue out of pride and it twisted her.' He paused to take another sip of brandy and put down his glass with seeming concentration. It was clear that he was approaching a climax in what he had to say. 'She was a Jenkins before she married.'

'A Jenkins?'

'Sister to Amos Jenkins who farms up the valley from the Peters' place.'

'Do they keep in touch?'

The old man's eyes expressed unmistakable satisfaction. 'Oh, yes. They are a tightly-knit clan, the Jenkinses. She visits every week on her free day. I've never known her miss.'

It was a small piece, not vital, perhaps, but it fitted.

Martin got to his feet and walked heavily to the door without another word. Wycliffe sat on for a few minutes longer and the silence in the bar was unbroken. Outside the dancers were applauding.

He had difficulty in making his way through the crowd, back to the school. The door of the café was open and the widow woman was standing on the step, taking the air. She pretended not to see him.

Chapter Nine

It was getting to be a habit, strolling along the quay on his way to the school. A scrawled poster outside the newsagent read:

ISLAND MURDERS
ARREST IMMINENT

That was how the press had translated his guarded statement. He bought his tobacco and thought that the shopkeeper looked at him with an apprehensive air. He was a thorn in the flesh; something to be got rid of as soon as possible, even though the removal might be painful.

Friday. He had been on the island since the previous Sunday night. Charlie Martin, standing outside his ticket office, acknowledged him curtly.

They all seemed to be telling him, 'Get it over!'

When he arrived at the school Jimmy Gill was there. 'You'll want to see this, it's just come through from forensic by phone.'

It was a preliminary report on the clothing which had been submitted for examination. Vince Peters' saxe-blue corduroy coat and trousers, Jackie Martin's Harris tweed jacket and Crimplene trousers. Nothing of note on the corduroys. Martin's trousers had been snagged in two places on the right leg and one of the snags yielded a minute fragment of red rust. There were also traces of powdered rust adhering to the material just below the pocket, also on the right side. Two fragments of rust had been recovered from the jacket, one from the pocket flap and one from inside the pocket itself. Faint traces of blood had been detected on the lining of the jacket in two places and the blood had been identified as human and belonging to group O.

'That clinches it so far as the girl is concerned,' Gill said.

Wycliffe was obstinately silent and sullen.

But Gill would never forget the next two hours and, as far as the squad was concerned, the events of those two hours would pass into legend. It began with a telephone call which Wycliffe made to Dr Ross. Gill did not hear what was said but he was in Wycliffe's office when the doctor rang back and he heard one side of that conversation. Wycliffe's manner was subdued, not to say grim.

'Thank you, doctor. I'm most grateful. You understand that I don't want the ambulance to arrive until . . . No, exactly. We want to make it as easy as possible . . . As you say, a tragedy.'

Wycliffe dropped the receiver onto its rest.

'What's on?'

'I've arranged for Jackie's father to be taken into hospital.'

'Does that mean . . . ?'

'Yes.'

'Who are you sending?'

'I'm going myself.'

'Then I'll go with you.'

'No, I'm taking Jordan, it will be . . .' He was going to say, kinder, but changed his mind and substituted, 'I want you here.'

He looked at his watch. 'Time I was going. I want you to send a car in half an hour.'

Down below, on the wharf, a queue was forming at the ticket office for boat trips. Brenda Luke would be there, pulling in the money for Charlie Martin and his syndicate. Charlie was in his usual place for this time of day, sitting on his particular bollard, keeping an eye on things. The boats were clustered round the steps waiting for their quotas. It was a fresh morning with puffy white clouds sailing in a blue sky before a stiff north-westerly breeze. It was calm enough in the harbour but outside the trippers would get their money's worth.

Jordan was waiting for him in the control room, dressed in plain clothes. He looked down at the grey worsted. 'I thought it might be better if . . .'

'Of course, you're quite right.'

Together they walked down the slope from the school on to the quay. Only Charlie Martin took any notice and he followed them with his eyes. As they drew level he made a slight movement of his shoulders which could have been interpreted as resignation.

'I feel sorry for the old man,' Jordan said. 'It'll be a terrible shock to him.'

'He knows.'

'You think so?'

'I'm sure of it.'

Jordan looked at him doubtfully but said nothing.

Wycliffe recognized two reporters outside the post office and they acknowledged him cheerfully. 'Anything for us, superintendent?'

He shook his head.

They arrived at the Tower House. Wycliffe paused on the step, he seemed to be hesitating about some course of action. At last he said, 'In spite of everything, I want you to stay here.'

'But the whole idea . . . It would come better from me . . .'

'Do as you're told!' Wycliffe knocked on the door and there was a considerable delay before it was opened.

Nellie Martin stood in the little hall, dressed in her old tweed coat. She seemed to have gone even thinner and her face was drawn and white. 'I was just going out.' But she stood aside for Wycliffe to come in and closed the door behind him. He followed her into the kitchen where the old man's chair was empty and the stove had not been lit.

'Your husband not down yet?'

'He's not well this morning, worse than usual.'

'I'm sorry.'

She was moving about the kitchen doing apparently pointless things, picking up a cup and putting it down again, pushing a chair a bit further under the table, straightening a mat with her foot . . . But Wycliffe noticed that she kept one hand in the pocket of her old coat.

'Jackie?'

She looked at him sharply. 'Up in his room.'

A pause during which they could hear people talking as they passed by outside.

'What are you here for?'

'I think you know.'

'You haven't brought his clothes?'

'No.'

She said nothing for a while but went on with her restless prowling, then she turned on him suddenly. 'I don't care for myself.' And she added after a moment, 'You know that, don't you?'

'Yes, I know.'

Another lengthy silence.

'What I've had I shall never miss.'

'No.'

'It's only the boy I care about.' Her voice faltered and he thought that she would break down. It would have been for the best, but she got control of herself again. 'It was his clothes?'

'Yes.'

The silence this time lasted longer. Through the lace blinds Wycliffe could see people walking past. A faint call from somewhere upstairs and she jerked her head upwards. 'It's him,' and gave a contemptuous little twist to her lips. 'He can wait.'

It was obvious that she had not made up her mind what she would do and the smallest gesture or word out of place might precipitate a crisis. He was glad that he had kept Jordan outside. It was his responsibility.

'You wouldn't lie to me – not about something like that?' Her expression was almost pleading.

'No.'

She stared at him as though trying to see into his mind. 'No.'

She stopped by one of the windows. Tourists were

trooping past on their way to the boats. 'You've got Freddie Jordan out there.'

'He's out there, yes.'

She continued to peer through the blind. 'There are two kinds in this world, aren't there?'

'Two kinds?'

'The ones who suffer and the ones who make others suffer. Look at them out there!' She turned away from the window. 'He would never have let the boy alone. He *knew*.'

'Vince Peters?'

She did not bother to answer that. 'I asked him what he was going to do and he said, "Jackie must tell them himself".'

'So you shot him.'

She nodded. 'I shot him.' She put her hand to her forehead in a curious gesture as though to brush away a fly or some other source of irritation.

'You went to see him on the way to visit your brother, is that it?'

'I took the gun out of the drawer and loaded it, then I went up to his room.' She was staring at nothing with unblinking eyes. 'The funny thing was he didn't seem to mind – he just sat there. I couldn't understand it . . .'

'He was suffering too – an incurable disease.'

She glanced at him sharply for a moment then the glazed look came over her eyes once more. 'So much the better for him.'

Another weak cry from upstairs.

'Shouldn't you go to your husband?'

She shook her head.

'He'll be looked after.'

'Do you think I care about him? He's nothing to me. He's never been a man, even before he was took sick . . .' Her eyes came alive again. 'You know he's not Jackie's father?'

'No, I didn't know.'

She nodded. 'Nobody knows. I kept the secret but if it hadn't been for the harm it would have done to the boy I would have shouted it from the housetops. Do you understand?'

'Yes.'

She laughed bitterly. 'You think you do.'

The letterbox rattled and the postman dropped something through which plopped on to the mat.

'Do you know Nicky Marsden?'

Wycliffe nodded. 'I know him.'

'A drunken sot who tried to show himself to young girls. He was Jackie's father.' She turned on him so abruptly that he was startled. 'Now do you understand?'

'I think so.'

'I'm guilty *because of what it did to Jackie*. For more than twenty years I've tried to pay the price but it was never enough.' She jerked her head upwards. 'Why do you think I've looked after him all these years? But you can't wipe out a living sin.'

She was back at the window, looking out. 'Don't they ever cheat or lie? Don't they ever *sin*? Don't those women out there . . . ?' She broke off and turned towards him again. 'But they don't have to pay, do they?'

She resumed her restless perambulation round the room but as she came close to the door, and before he could stop her, she slipped out into the hall. By the time he got there she was two or three steps up the stairs and she had the gun in her hand, pointed at him. 'Stay where you are! If you come any nearer . . . You know that I can.'

He was frightened but he managed to keep fear from his voice. 'How did you learn to use a gun?'

She laughed. 'Nicky Marsden taught me. He got hold of a gun from a Yankee officer and used to show off to the girls. I only tried it once or twice but I remembered.'

He tried to sound calm, reasonable. 'You will only make matters very much worse. Jackie can be helped.'

'Jackie can only be helped by me. It's always been the same.'

'That's not true!'

She shrugged as though the point was not worth discussion and then took another step backwards up the stairs. He moved towards her and she fired. He felt a sudden, numbing pain his arm and put his hand to the spot. Already the blood had soaked through his thin jacket. He kept his feet but she had disappeared up the stairs. Jordan burst in. Wycliffe made to follow but at that moment there was a crash somewhere upstairs followed by what sounded like a muted explosion. Jordan, white faced, was looking at the blood running from Wycliffe's arm and trickling down on to the floor. Whatever his intention he had come between Wycliffe and the stairs.

'After her, you fool! I'm all right!'

But though Jordan tried he was too late. Already the flames could be heard and the walls were lit by an ugly, flickering glow. 'That stairs is like a chimney

– there's not a hope.' And, indeed, the flames were roaring now, drowning other sounds. Then came a shot, an interval, then another.

'The old man!' Wycliffe shouted. 'She hasn't bothered with him!'

With his good arm he wrenched open the front door. They heard the joyous whoosh of flame due to the added draught and slammed the door behind them. At that moment Gill arrived with two men in a police car.

'A ladder for the first floor!' Wycliffe shouted but Jordan was off like a sprinter to his house which was no more than a hundred yards away. 'Help him! Don't just stand there!' A constable went after Jordan.

By a miracle they got the old man out alive. The fire which had started on the first landing had licked up through the staircase before starting to eat its way through the woodwork into the rooms. So he was put into the ambulance after all.

Wycliffe refused to go to the hospital and was bandaged by the ambulance men on the spot, strapped up like a chicken ready for the oven.

The Tower House continued to burn. A great pillar of smoke rose up from it and was whisked away by the wind over the harbour and out to sea. There was nothing anybody could do. The fire brigade played their hoses to no effect and the police kept back the crowds who preferred this to the boats or the beach. Then the lead cupola started to melt and hot metal bullets showered down, spattering on the ground like hailstones and forcing the fire brigade back as well.

* * *

Wycliffe and Gill sat in the headmaster's room at the school. Wycliffe was trying to light his pipe with one hand and Gill knew better than to offer help. From the window he could see the boats gathered round the steps for afternoon trips and the tourists being helped aboard. Charlie Martin was sitting on his bollard. From a distance even the Tower House looked much as usual except that its cupola was missing. The firemen were still there.

Gill said, 'She took a five gallon drum to the shop yesterday and had it filled with paraffin. The boy who works there carried it home for her on a trolley.'

Wycliffe did not answer. He had managed to light his pipe and he puffed away, staring at nothing.

'Apparently she uses quite a lot of paraffin and the shopkeeper didn't think anything of it . . . She must have had it on the first landing – ready.'

Wycliffe still did not speak. He had decided to go home by sea that afternoon. He would leave Jimmy Gill to tie up the loose ends. He could not rid himself of the thought that had he handled the case differently Jackie Martin and his mother might still be alive.

When, at 4.25, the *Islander* gave a warning blast on her siren, he was halfway down the slope to the quay. Jordan was with him, carrying his bag. At the bottom of the gangway Charlie Martin was waiting. He pressed a bottle-shaped package under Wycliffe's good arm. 'Look after it, Mr Wycliffe, it's a drop of the good stuff. Come back and spend a holiday – you'll be very welcome.'

He stood on deck while they cast off and watched

while the *Islander* passed through the pier heads and started to pitch gently in the swell. Soon the island grew smaller and he could no longer distinguish the harbour entrance. He knew then that he would never go back.

THE END